HE GATHERED HIS POWER
IN A FRIGHTENING DANCE...

Frightening because Daremo could feel the power. Feel it as if he were piling weights on Daremo's soul.

The man's body moved in the incredible dance of death: earth, water, wood, metal, and fire; dragon, tiger, chicken, horse, monkey, snake, falcon, lizard, eagle, and bear; the movement, the strategy, the spirit. He had gone beyond his earthly muscles. The spark of Archer's mental attack had taken him to hell. And in hell, the fire was limitless and eternal.

He screamed and charged Daremo, his hands out, his fingers clawed. Daremo wrenched his body away desperately. He scrambled out between the wall and the attacker, whose hands went *into* the pagoda, ripping through as if the walls were cardboard.

Then the side of his hand smashed across Daremo's jaw...

THE YEAR OF THE NINJA series
by Wade Barker

Dragon Rising
Lion's Fire
Serpent's Eye
Phoenix Sword

Published by
WARNER BOOKS

PHOENIX SWORD

The Year of the Ninja Master: Winter

Wade Barker

WARNER BOOKS

A Warner Communications Company

There are three thousand and nine hundred islands that make up Japan. Everything in the book exists on at least one of them. All the lore and ritual is factual, but, as usual, the language is all messed up. Void where prohibited by law. Some assembly required.

WARNER BOOKS EDITION

Warner Books, Inc.
666 Fifth Avenue
New York, N.Y. 10103

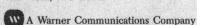 A Warner Communications Company

Printed in the United States of America

First Printing: January, 1986

10 9 8 7 6 5 4 3 2 1

TO BILL AND KAREN PALMER PALMER (SIC)

"Don't just want to write what they want to publish—make them want to publish what you want to write."

Acknowledgments

To the others responsible:
Al Sirois, Jeff Rovin,
Jim Frost, and Richard Meyers

PART ONE
TENGU

Let justice be done, though the heavens fall.
Lord Mansfield

1

How many times can a man die?
  Why bother to ask such questions?
  How many times can a man die?

He could no longer control his mind consciously. His thoughts flowed unceasingly, as if poured into his mind. Inside they coursed, twisting in a never-ending circle, drifting in a gentle whirlpool.

Images presented themselves to his mind's eye. He was a fetus, born once of woman—but he did not remember that; he only had others' words for that. *This* he could experience, could remember, and would never forget. This time he was being born of the dirt. He was in the ground, buried in a fetal position. He was full-grown, but still a fetus being born again.

How many times can a man die? More than once, that was certain. But that was not the question, not the *right* question. The right question was: *why did a man die?*

Because they wanted him to die. They did not want him dead, but wanted him to die so he could be born again in their image. The one born of woman had to die so the one of the dirt could live.

That was why they had returned him to his maker—the earth. Ashes to ashes, earth to earth, what is a man's worth? Ashes to ashes, dust to dust, he would do as he must. He would die and be born again . . . or he would die, simply die, and serve another.

Images flowed; things he recognized and some he did not. His life flashed before his eyes. The life before *and* the life after. He saw what he had experienced and that which he would experience. But he did not know that then. He only knew he saw images he could not recognize. And it terrified him. It would leave his eyes wide and unseeing, his mouth slack and drooling. He wanted to scream but the dirt held his mouth closed like cement. He screamed anyway—in his throat and in his mind.

He panicked. He ordered his fingers to claw, his arms to flail, his legs to run. The orders were ambushed by a man who stood in full armor—the Kote, the Do, the Nodowa, the Haidate, the Sendan-no-ita, the Hato-o-no-ita. He blocked them as if they were wild animals of the wood, sending them back into the forest by the pure force of his will.

He recognized the man. He was happy to see him. His horror, his panic left him. The man was himself. He lay in the dirt, his head two feet beneath the earth's surface, motionless. He viewed the images calmly now, reading to himself. Now he was as a father, watching his children play their blood-curdling games of make-believe as he read scholarly works to himself. The images were mere fantasy now. The words were real.

One: Do not think dishonestly.

Two: The Way is training.

Three: Become acquainted with every art.

Four: Know the Ways of all professions.

Five: Distinguish between gain and loss in worldly matters.

Six: Develop intuitive judgment and understanding for everything.

Seven: Perceive those things which cannot be seen.

Eight . . .

Eight? There was no eight. Not yet. For him there were only seven.

There were more. There was an eight and there was a nine. But he could go no further. He was at seven now, buried in the ground. *Perceive those things which cannot be seen.* Above him was his world just over his head. He could see that world now, clearer than it had ever been. Everything, from blades of grass to the vast oceans, and the even more vast skies. And beyond . . . ?

No.

How like blades of grass were humans. How like the sky, how like the seas. The harmony was clear to him. Was that the unperceived? Was he free? Could he rise from his grave now?

No. It was clear to him even as he hoped. The oneness of all nature was not unperceived. It existed always and was perceived always. It was not always acknowledged, that was all. No. There was more yet to discover. He did not know what it was, but he knew that it had to be.

He thought. That was all that was left him. He decided that to learn what he did not know he would have to learn what he did know. Who was he? He had no name. It had been taken from him upon his burial. If he rose from his grave, he would have another. All he knew was that he existed. For now, that had to be enough.

Where was he? Buried. Yes. He could admit that to himself. He had no fear now. They did not want him babbling, insane. They wanted him to remember. They had buried him in the ritual so that he could perceive the unseen. They had smiled and nodded, knowing what that was, knowing what that was like. And he went to his grave knowing that they had gone and returned. If they could do it . . . could he? He existed. *That had to be enough.*

Where. *Where?* Did the place make a difference? He felt it did. He could have been in Europe, he could have been in Africa, in the Americas, in the Arctics. He was not. He was in Asia, the Far East. He was in Japan. He was on the island of Nemuro. He was *in* the island of Nemuro.

This is what death is like. The earth all around me. The worms and insects crawling over me. The roots of the plants around me. Parts of the earth—decaying, disintegrating—part of nature.

No, think! *Think of who you are and what you are*

and where you are. You exist. You have not gone on. You have not left the hollow shell. You are *the hollow shell. You are in Nemuro. You lie under the ground, weightless, as if floating in space. You breathe. You live. Just barely, but just so.*

In this state, near the gate of death, you can appreciate, if not understand, what it is to be alive.

Is that what I must perceive? No. Who am I, where am I, what am I? When am I? What year is it? No, it is not forever. It is not eternity. Time *does* have meaning here. I was to be buried for a certain length of time. I had to perceive or else die. But time was a factor. I am to be dug up. They will come for me, and they will know just by looking at me whether I have succeeded or failed. Or have died.

Think. When is it? It has meaning. What year is it?

Nineteen-forty. It is nineteen-forty. The world is at war. For those on the battlefields and in the ovens, it is soon over: A few seconds that seem endless, a realization that is far greater than the pain, a torrent of overwhelming emotions and images, then peace, bliss, and disintegrating death.

But only the flesh and bones twist and eventually disappear. Only the shell. The essence is already gone to serve another. But if those few seconds are drawn out to minutes, then hours, then days . . .

He, the buried one, had to die that long.

He saw twisted, tortured souls dancing in Hades, dancing in woe, shrieking and crying until the wailing became song. These were not the ghosts of those who had died. They were the souls of those who were to die, tortured, in incomprehensible torment.

He saw the shame of their defeat. He saw the horror in their loss of pride. And he saw other people, those who lived in an underworld of their own, mutate beneath their shame, the shame that was greater than any physical punishment.

The dancing demons faded from his mind's eye. Instead he saw the brilliance of the sky, the light of the waters, the truth of all things. He heard laughter and turned to find its source. He looked all around him. There was nothing there, but the laughter continued. He looked below his feet, to the earth, but the laughter was not coming from there. Finally, he looked up.

There, in the sky, was the mountain. He scaled its snowy peaks and beyond until he came to the patch of wood. He looked into the limbs of the ash-white tree that was rooted in eternity and saw the tengu perched there. The tengu which was laughing at him. The tengu that was himself.

"The truth of all things!" The tengu laughed. "What do you know of that?"

The tengu was like all tengus: winged with a long beaklike nose. It wore a small black hat to cover its baldness. The buried one simple stared at it.

"Oh, the old silent treatment, eh?" the mountain deity said, its head sliding back on its birdlike neck. Suddenly it pointed at the buried one, smiling.

"You are Hama," it said. "The vastness of the ocean, the peace of the shore. You are Hama, little one."

Hama looked down at himself. He was both the

fourteen-year-old buried in the dirt and the round, bald man who sought to kill his master.

"When they ask," the tengu said, "you can tell them it came to you in a vision."

He was gone from the mountain. He was the old man. He was the mountain creature living in the tree. He was the boy buried in the ground of a tiny island as his elders trained to kill the roundeyes. He too must kill, but he must kill his own people. That's what he was training for, why he was buried in the dirt.

Hama was the beach. *Hama* meant beach. It was, as the tengu had said, the vastness of the sea, the serenity of the shore. Who could walk on a beach at night, alone, and not think of the great mysteries? The mystery of life . . . of love. It was—he was—Hama.

It should have ended there, but it did not. He was more than his name. He was a creation, a miracle—as all humans are, but a miracle shaped. He was the child, even younger now. He was in training even as he became aware. He could not remember before the age of three, but there were distant feelings of love and pain.

They loved him, but they always caused him pain. *They had to; he deserved it.*

That was automatic. He could not relive the pain without remembering the teachings, especially the most important teaching: they *had* to cause him pain.

Not for him the toys of childhood. The sword became his toy. But he could not play with the sword. They had to teach him, even before he knew what learning was, that he could not play with the blade. It was given to him as soon as he was born. . . .

He remembered his father used to tell him that he, the child, had slept with the blade every night from the very day he was born. Hama didn't believe him but did not say so. He would never say so. His father struck him.

"You don't believe me."

"No, sir."

His father struck him again. "You *don't* believe me."

"No, sir, I believe you."

"You do *not!*" Hama was struck again, across the face, with an open palm, hard.

"I believe you, sir."

Hama was struck in the stomach with a fist. He nearly collapsed. He centered his energy, did not lose his footing, and stood.

"You do not believe me, boy," his father said. "Your words can lie, but your face cannot."

"Yes, sir. I do not believe it, sir."

His father suddenly kicked him across the jaw. Hama never saw the leg coming. He crashed to the ground, blinded by shock, and then the pain.

"But you *must* believe me," his father hissed into his ear. "It is the truth."

"I believe you," Hama gasped.

He was struck again. He was losing consciousness. He heard his father's words as he fell into the blackness.

"You cannot use words. You must *believe* me."

Hama finally understood. He heard his own words in the darkness. "He must see it, not hear it."

Hama was three. Hama was in training as he became aware. His first tangible memory was of the tree branch. The tengu laughed at him as he remembered. He was perched on the tree branch high in the air. His father sat against the tree trunk.

"Come to me, son," he said. Hama started to crawl. "No," his father said. "You must walk. You must stand and walk toward me. Come, son. Come to your father who loves you."

As Hama stood, he remembered walking, first across the floor, then immediately across planks stretched between stones on the ground. He remembered falling from the plank and crying on the ground for many minutes. But every day he would be back on the plank, with his father calling to him.

"Come, son. Come to your father who loves you."

And he would walk across the plank to the man's arms. And his father would hug him. Then he would send his son back to the other end of the plank.

"Turn around. Kneel. Sit. Stand. Jump." Hama would do as he was told. He had to. If he fell, then he would be on the ground, where he would cry until his father put him back on the plank. Then he would walk, kneel, sit, stand, and jump. His father would hug him and raise the plank.

Soon he was traversing the limbs of a tall tree. Kneeling, sitting, standing, and jumping. And if ever he slipped, he would fall. Or he would grab onto the branch. But he would not crawl back on. His father wouldn't let him. His father would kick him off again. Not to fall, but to hang. He would have to hang the rest of the day and much of the night. He would hang until his arms ached and his muscles spasmed. Then he would hang some more.

He would hang until he felt sure his father would no longer be awake. He would hang until he was absolutely certain his father was in bed, asleep. Then he would drop through the night, praying the ground was not so far that it would kill him or break his limbs. He would often fall asleep right there, in tears, terrified that his father would beat him if he discovered the boy had not remained hanging from the limb.

He would cry himself to sleep, praying to the gods and demanding of himself that he be awakened before dawn so he could climb back up the tree and crawl to the end of the limb, so that his father could find him still hanging come the morning. But on the next day it was as if the previous day had not happened. His father would call him for the morning meal and they would start anew.

Even so, every time he slipped, he would hang until he could bear it no more and then still pray to awaken before his father. Soon his prayers were answered. He could hang all day and all night, but by then, he would never fall unless his father tripped him. And they had left the tree. Now the boy walked a thin branch across a chasm. The drop was fifty feet into a roaring torrent.

He would walk, kneel, sit, roll, stand, and jump across the knotted, uneven branch as the water raged below. He did it in the rain and the snow. If he slipped, he would hold on until his father came to him the following morning, when they'd begin again. He would do it until he no longer slipped and fell.

On that day he stood before his father proudly. His father pushed him back and tripped him. Hama fell and held onto the branch.

The next morning he found two tall sticks with a rope tied between their crowns where his father had been. His father was now some ways off. He shouted for his son not to return home until he could jump over the rope.

Hama tried. He ran and jumped, throwing his body through the air, but he could not clear it. The hemp scraped along his chest and thighs until he was on the other side. He did not feel the pain until he had landed on the dew-kissed grass. He looked at his front in amazement. It was torn, as if he had been flayed. He held his blood-stained hands out and looked to the rope.

It was not rope but brambles wrapped tightly together until they appeared to be rope. It was essentially one long thorn.

His eyes blinded by tears, Hama threw himself back and forth across the rope barrier, astonished at his father's devious cleverness. His breath escaped his throat and clenched teeth in gasps as he tore his flesh back and forth across the thin obstruction. He jumped and dove, never completely clearing it, until he lay in an exhausted heap by the cliff's edge.

The frustration was enormous, even greater than the pain. He would sail through the air, until he was certain he would clear the rope, only to feel the pinlike prick

on his side, his back, his rib, or his waist, his leg or
foot. And with each jump, his muscles became weaker.
Still, he would throw himself up again and again, his
spirit refusing to let his body fail.

But it did. He lay, certain that he was paralyzed and
choking to death. He lay until he felt his father's warm
hands on his shoulders. That gave him the strength to
rise yet again. The strength seemed to flow through the
man into him. They walked together to the dark house.
And in that dark house, he learned.

His starving mind soaked up the information his
father gave him. His exhausted body accepted the new
posture and breathing techniques without balk or com-
plaint. Without knowing it, he learned to harness his
inner strength. He learned the three interior arts during the nights after the days of leaping over the ever-
rising thorn rope. When he was giddy from shock and
loss of blood, his father would reshape his pliant thoughts.

As he sat cross-legged on the floor, his eyes closed,
forcing his body to accept a new reality of breathing and
existing, he didn't even listen to the words his father
chanted. But he heard them.

"*Ai Uchi.*"

"*Hanshi minna imasu.*"

"*Hanshi zembu imasu.*"

"*Kessh'te wasuremasu.*"

"*Ai Uchi, Hanshi imasu minna, Hanshi zembu imasu,
kessh'te wasuremasu.*"

The next day, and all the days that followed, he
cleared the rope. He stood again before his father, his
back to the chasm he had walked across, and then

leaped over. His father pushed him over the edge of the cliff.

He fell and fell, until he hit the boiling current. It swept him down. He fought it with all his strength, utilizing the breathing lessons he had assimilated to keep from drowning. He made it to the surface alive but then the rushing torrent swept him far out to sea. When he was finally able to break away from the current, the shore was just a distant horizon.

Hama swam. He moved through the water until he reached the shore. He lay on the sand like a beached whale—another meaning for his name. He lay until his father struck him with a stick. He looked up to see his parent's angry countenance.

"You have failed," his father said. "You will be punished."

With that, his father walked to the house. Hama followed. In his small, windowless room, his father tied him in a sitting position on the floor. His arms were bent high up his back and secured there. His legs were also bent and secured. Then his limbs were secured to one another. His father looked him in the eye as he stood by the entrance to the spartan, rice-paper walled room.

"If you are not free by morning, you will be punished again," he said.

Hama was not free by morning. His father came in and beat him with a bamboo stick as he sat, cringing, on the floor. The man looked down at his morose, welt-covered son.

"I have no blade," he said. "I cannot cut you loose. I have torn my fingers with worry for you. I cannot untie you." He leaned down and dislocated Hama's shoulders and hips. Hama was stunned by the pain, but the ropes seemed to fall off him. His father's expression was one of disgust as he dragged his numb son to the cliff's edge and hurled him over.

Again Hama swam, and again his father collected him and tied him in his room. They repeated the ritual until Hama could run from the sea and appear for the morning meal without a mark of rope upon him. On that day, his father brought him to the cliff's edge.

"Dive," he said. Hama dove into the current. When he broke the water's surface again, an arrow shot into the liquid, just missing him. He looked up to see his father firing arrows at him from a longbow. He dove deep, until the arrows no longer came near him. He swam underwater until he could bear it no more. Another arrow broke the waves as he reappeared. He dove and swam underwater again. He repeated the action until he was out of range.

But when he again approached the shore, his father, his father's bow, and his father's arrows were waiting for him. He was forced to dive and swim underwater again and again to avoid becoming his father's target. Every day their actions would be repeated, the arrows sometimes scratching the boy's skin, until Hama was no longer a target. He would dive deep and swim far.

On that day he faced his father again, but his father had dropped the bow and arrows and waved frantically for the boy to come ashore. Hama could not believe what he saw when he approached his father. The man's normally placid face was twisted with deep emotion and horror.

"Your mother is stricken ill," he said. "You must get medicine for her or she will die." Hama gasped. "The medicine is in Hanzo." Fifty miles away. "You must go and get it and come back. Tomorrow will be too late."

It never occurred to Hama that this might not be the truth. *"You* must *believe me!"* He ran as fast as he could. He ran until his legs gave out, and he fell to the ground so hard his knees were torn. He ran until he could run no longer, then he walked until his feet were bloodied. He walked until he collapsed. A passing cart gave him a ride to Hanzo, but from there, he ran back.

He ran and he ran. Until his chest was a furnace and his throat raw from breathing. He arrived home with the sun midway in the eastern sky. His father walked across the front yard to greet him. He was without expression. He took the packet of herbs his son held up.

"It is mid-morning," he said flatly. "Your mother is dead." He threw the medicine to the ground and walked away.

Hama ran into the house, crying and calling out his mother's name. He stumbled into her room, but she was not there. He fell upon her empty bamboo bed mat and lost consciousness.

When he awoke the house was dark and empty. All he found was a note from his father saying that his mother's funeral was in Hanzo the following morning. If he did not appear, his mother's spirit would walk the Earth, never resting in peace.

Hama ran to Hanzo. He did not stop. He harnessed all he had learned, holding himself in such a way that he could breathe in as much air as he needed. His swim-hardened legs held him aloft. He ignored any discomfort. He ran all the way to Hanzo in a little over six hours.

Even so, it was too much for his body to accept. He lost consciousness again as he reached the doctor's stall where he had first been directed for the medicine. When he awoke, he was back home, his mother feeding him tea and miso soup. His father was in the doorway to his room.

"She has recovered," he said. "I was mistaken. I have not a doctor's training in these things."

Hama later discovered that he had spent many days in delirium. When he could again stand, he sought out his father to apologize. He discovered his parent in his own room, seated upon the floor, his back to him. Hama walked toward him. Suddenly his father whirled around, his arm lashing out. Hama fell back, his ankle cut. He lay in the doorway looking at the sharp sword in his father's hand.

"I do not want to hear you!" his father seethed.

But each day his mother would approach the boy and say, "Go to your father." But each time the man would whirl at the first sound, the first sign, the first signal, and cut his son with the gleaming sword. It wasn't until Hama could enter and walk silently that his father would let him near.

On that day, his mother came to Hama and again said, "Go to your father." In his father's room, the man sat, but around him were delicate vases. Hama had to walk among these works of pottery without touching them or making a sound. It was many more days before he could approach his father again.

And on that day his mother told him, "Go to your father... touch not the floor."

Hama tried to walk across the vase tops. He would fall among broken ceramics and be cut every time he made noise. It was months before he could see his father's face again. He did not know he could lose so much blood and still live. But finally he was able to approach and circle his father silently. On that day, his father merely threw the sword to his son and attacked him.

The father used another sword that lay before him at his feet. The sword was long, sharp, and straight. For days he defeated his son, cutting him about the hands and arms. When Hama learned to protect those limbs, his father attacked his torso and legs. After many weeks of training, Hama was finally able to protect the rest of his body. Only then did his father throw his sword away.

He quickly disarmed his son and beat him unmercifully. He struck and kicked the boy. Every blow Hama threw, he blocked. He hurled Hama about the room until the boy began to understand how his own body worked. Then suddenly, his father changed strategy. He would lock Hama's limbs, choke the boy, and render him helpless with a touch, until the child began to understand that too.

And then the boy fought back. But for every hold he

managed to complete upon his father, his parent escaped it. He kept out of the boy's range with silent leaps and acrobatics. Soon enough, Hama was matching his father's tumbles and trying to stymie the adult with grips and attacks of his own device.

For a time, his father countered these inventions with ease. But just as Hama was getting closer to catching his father, the man threw a stick at him. This was different from the branches Hama would walk across. This was a straight, polished staff that was six feet long. For weeks, the two fought with those until Hama began to parry his father's blows. On that day, the parent suddenly tore the end of his own staff aside to reveal a blade with which he cut his son's arm deeply.

Hama lost the use of that arm for weeks. At first he fell into a second delirium from loss of blood. When again he could fight, his father handed him a pole with a spear tip. The spear tip had a hook at its base. For weeks the two sparred with that weapon until Hama could again hold his own. Then came the chains.

That was the worst. The chains initially had weights on their ends. Later they sprouted blades. It took months to even begin to use them with any degree of proficiency. And then the stack was shuffled. One day he had the sword and his father the spear; the next he had a staff and his father the chain. It went on and on in all variety of combinations.

Years went by. He grew without knowing it, and without the knowledge of childhood. He fought through his life until the day his father threw his weapons down.

He simply stopped fighting, backed away from his son, and threw his weapons to the floor. Without a word he turned and walked through the house.

Hama followed his father across the hardwood floors, past the teak wall supports and the rice paper expanses. He followed until he noticed his mother in a side doorway. He stopped to look at her. His father continued out the door.

Her face was flushed and her eyes red with emotion. It was the first time he had seen his mother this way. He went to her with concern. She stopped his approach by holding out a bag of uncooked rice.

"Take this," she said. "Eat it all as you follow him."

Hama followed his father into the countryside, dazed. They walked for two days and a night. They walked until the rice bag was empty and three men stood before them. Only then did his father turn to him.

"You are ready," he said. "Do not fail."

The four men buried the fourteen-year-old in the glorious sunrise.

He didn't know how he knew, but he did. He knew all this and more. He knew the unspoken in terms no words could convey. He knew who, where, when, and what he was. He was the tengu—no wonder it had laughed at him. He was becoming the yamabushi—the warrior priest, the monk of the mountains. He was being trained as the samurais had been trained, and beyond. He was being trained as the ninja were trained, and beyond.

He lay for days in the dirt, under the ground, losing

his mind and regaining it as the men above prayed to, and for, him.

He never felt himself rising from the ground on midnight of the last day. He felt no ascent of any kind. One reality, he was buried, the next, he was not. When he opened his eyes, the three knew they had succeeded.

The fourth, his father, was not there.

As far as Hama really knew, he could still be buried. After that burial, life was but a dream. Life became no stranger than what he had felt planted in the ground those hundred and sixty-eight hours.

Following were thirty-four thousand, nine hundred and forty-four more hours in the company of the three men who had buried him. They took him to the land of the tengu, to a Buddhist temple. There he sat with them and participated in a different form of fighting.

He learned to read and write—not just Japanese, but Chinese, Russian, and English. He learned mathematics, chemistry, and biology. He learned philosophy and meditation, spending hours perfecting his sense of inner wisdom. His teachers were less violent, but no less cunning than Hama's father.

He would sit alone in a room for many hours, then the teachers would enter and demand that he tell them their every movement inside that room. He became adept at identifying sounds. From then on, he studied every craft—medicine, farming, the legal system, and religion.

He would then go for walks with his teachers, discussing his education all the while. After many hours of hiking, the teacher would find fault with something he had said and demand that Hama stay away from both the temple and the area towns for days at a time. The young man soon became equally adept at living off the land.

Each time he returned to the temple, it would be locked or guarded a different way. And each time he had to devise a new way of entering. After that, the lessons became more personal. Each teacher gave Hama the benefit of their experience. They taught him tricks no one could find in books.

Then one day it all ended. Just like that. One day Hama awoke to find the temple empty. He wandered around its interior until he noticed a pattern to the stones and small rocks in the courtyard. One patch actually made up, constellation-style, the symbol for the word *koko*, or here.

Digging beneath it, Hama found a message directing him to the island of Ogami. Never thinking of questioning the order, Hama spent a few days preparing for the trip. He researched the island. It was two hundred and fifty miles away, off the west coast of Hokkaido, the northern uppermost island of the Japanese "mainland." Two hundred and fifty miles across the Sea of Japan from it was the Soviet Union. At this time of year, it would be very cold.

Hama dressed in Buddhist monk's trappings: a floor-length robe, with a wrapped cloth over one shoulder and under one arm. But beneath that he made sure his undergarments were plentiful and warm. He wrapped his feet in cloth that he tied in place until he had makeshift boots. Under his feet he placed cord sandals that he tied to his toes, heel, and ankles.

Although the temple was empty of people, the pantry was not bare. Hama prepared pills made of buckwheat and potato flour, wheat germ, and ground carrots—using grass as a firmative. He carried a small pouch of uncooked rice on his rope belt. Then he walked into the wood surrounding the temple.

He circled the place that had been his home for the last four years until he found a branch to his liking. From it he fashioned a six-foot-long makeshift staff. Walking stick in hand, he set out for Ogami. It was 1944.

In the south, the United States military was bombing Iwo Jima and preparing to invade both that and other volcano islands. But in the far north, the peasants knew little of war. Life for them went on as it had for centuries. The villages on the coasts were filled with fishermen. The villages inland, at the base of the mountain chains, were filled with rice farmers.

The two exchanged crops and catch, so the main meal, breakfast, lunch, and dinner, was rice with fish or fish with rice—depending upon where one lived. After a few days traveling in those circles, Hama was glad for the change in diet his pills could have afforded him had he chosen to eat them. But he knew the pills were for emergencies—for the times when he had to hide or wait.

Instead he traveled openly among the villages and their people, never offering his Buddhist services, but never turning any request away. Usually he would take payment for his work in food. But almost always, he could find decent sustenance at the many shrines that dotted the village paths, with or without priestly work.

He made his way toward Ogami carefully. He never hurried, but he never slowed, either. His passage was purposeful. The higher north he went, the colder it was. He soon became thankful he had researched the area so well. For many days his only shelters were the deserted shrines and temples he had carefully sought out on maps before he left.

He had passed Uchiura Bay on the southwest tip of Hokkaido and was making his way up the coast. When he finally arrived in Haboro—three-quarters up the large land mass, he found a willing boatman to take him to the tiny isle of Ogami.

"I'm only doing this because I'm a religious man," the boatman said. Hama was surprised he was saying anything, considering the cold. He should have remained silent in the sea wind, with his scarf wrapped around his face.

"Buddha bless you," Hama said.

"Save your blessings," the boatman said. "The Ogami people need them a lot more than I do."

Hama was tempted to question him further, but thought better of it. In one respect he didn't want to know... he wanted to discover whatever reason his teachers had sent him here himself. In another respect he didn't want to break his cover. Although he was, by all rights, an actual priest, he was also yamabushi—which made him both more and less than a priest. As far as he was presently concerned, however, he was in disguise. A Buddhist priest would not third-degree a boatman.

The island appeared ominous in the distance because of the gray sheet of sleeting mist that covered the area—as well as the boatman's tense words.

"Well, all I can say," the man continued as they neared, "is that I'm glad you're going there and not me."

"You are a most generous and honorable man," Hama said, complimenting him highly, "to bring me to this place in such weather."

"Like I said, priest, I'm a religious man. Anything I can do for these people I should. I couldn't live with myself otherwise. On the other hand, to their shore is as far as I'll go. From there, you . . . and them . . . are on your own."

The boatman pulled up to a deserted wharf. Hama noticed that not only were the dock's skiffs empty, they were in ill repair.

"My hopes and prayers go with you, priest," the boatman said anxiously, helping him out.

"And mine with you," Hama said. But his words fell on deaf ears. The boatman was already quickly moving away, back to the Haboro coastline. The warrior priest gripped his staff more tightly and turned to move inland.

Most of Ogami mirrored the disrepair of the wharf. Hama crossed a snow-covered road to find a line of deserted shacks. At first he thought they had been closed for the winter season, but he soon discovered that nothing was secured. The doors were unlocked, and the furniture and items inside showed that the cabins had been left quickly. Food, now frozen, was still on plates. Clothes fluttered across the floors in the vicious wind.

Hama moved away from the line of sheds and looked further inland. Through his squinting lids and the drift-strewn air, he could see a small temple up from the coastline road. Leaning heavily on his staff, he made his way toward it. As he walked, the snow sometimes coming up to his ankles, the coarse weather lessened. By the time he reached the stone wall and iron entry portal to the temple, it was almost an idyllic winter day.

The air was clean and crisp, almost invigorating if not for the deep chill. Everything seemed to stand out more sharply amid the pure white of the snow. Hama moved into the temple courtyard from under the two stone uprights and the double iron bar crossing them. The centerpiece of the yard was a twisted, gnarled tree. All around it were discarded grave markings and crumbling stone statues.

Hama shook his head in spite of himself. He was acting exactly as a Buddhist monk would. His first feeling upon seeing the strewn wood markers was one of piteous disgust. How could the deceased's descendants treat their memory this way? It was shameful to leave the teak tablets on the wooden stands so carelessly around. Each was inscribed with the name of the departed. By rights, they should be set in a small honorarium near the family house and prayed to daily.

Hama started to gather up the markers, paying no mind to the names on each. He slowed as he neared one of the statues, then stopped. It wasn't weather that had gouged and tipped the monuments this way, he noted. They looked as if they had been . . . attacked. As if they had been set upon and hacked at by a madman.

Hama stepped away, only to almost trip on something in the snow. Curious, he brushed the white stuff aside to find a wooden spike embedded in the frozen ground. He was about to leave it be when something else caught his eye. He kneeled down and tried to focus on the strange luminescence along the crown. It looked as if someone had hammered a bright silver nail into its flat top.

The yamabushi pulled the stake up and looked closely at the odd implement. He felt along the "nail"'s top. It wasn't a nail after all. It was ice. Hama frowned. How could a drop of water freeze so perfectly in the center of a wooden spike? Easy answer; it couldn't. Well, maybe . . . no, it wasn't possible.

Hama put the spike in his rope belt and continued to gather the tablets until he neared the trunk of the grand old tree. He placed all the markers at its base and straightened up to take another look around. The area was as eerily empty as before. Surveying the wharf area below him and examining the small temple and beyond, he saw that nothing stirred. Ogami was, so far, a ghost town.

Hama started to lean over to gather the markers again, but as he did so, something else caught the corner of his vision. He straightened to look into a knothole in the wide, tan, barkless tree trunk. There was something white in there. Snow, he thought, starting to lean again. No, he thought, straightening again. He peered carefully. A trick of the light, the sun reflecting off a smooth section of the tree's interior.

No. There was something distinct inside—something white that wasn't more of the tree or snow. Hama reached in, his hand completely filling the knothole. With careful patience he snaked his fingers around the smooth, cold end of . . . whatever it was.

Hama slowly pulled out a long, bleached white bone.

It was not an animal's bone, unless that was some big animal. A tangible chill sliced the nape of Hama's neck. The wind was blowing again. But as it coursed across the young man's neck and beyond, it brought a sound to his ears. A small, hardly perceptible noise—like the ghost of a forgotten bamboo wind chime.

It was the sound of . . . hollow rattling. Hama looked up into branches of the tree. A human skeleton sat there.

Hama entered the temple quickly. It was simply an open room. The only thing in it was an altar, seven feet wide, four feet deep, and ten feet tall. Various torn strips of prayers were tacked to it, as were rended photos of those passed on. Dead stalks of incense littered the surface, as did cracked, empty bowls—which once held a never-ending supply of food to honor the dead.

Hama placed all the grave markers there and walked away from the pitiful sight to examine the stake he had pulled up. He stood with his back to the altar, his face toward the courtyard, turning the spike over and over in his hands. Then, deliberately, he crouched and tapped the stake on the floor. The sound told him the wood was hollow. He now had no doubts that water had been poured into the hollowed-out stake.

He also had little doubt that he would find three more of these outside, under the snow, in a roughly rectangular pattern.

Two things made for a great ninja or yamabushi. One was the kind of training Hama had undergone. The other was insanity.

The girl leaped upon Hama without his having heard or seen her. She clawed for the stake, screeching unintelligibly into his ear. He bent over, sending her scrambling across his back and onto the floor. He jerked toward the altar and brought his staff around, gripping the spike as if it were a tanto blade.

Although he saw his attacker at the last moment, he was unable to prevent the tip of his stick from clouting her a good one across the jaw. She dove to the right, her chin leading. As she fell, Hama could clearly see her long, straight, dirty black hair, and her thin body in tattered rags.

She lay across the cold stone floor of the temple, her eyes unfocused, her blue lower lip cracked open and bleeding. She clawed across the floor toward the corner, crying and babbling in her stunned, pained state. Her kimono had once been pretty and whole, as she had been. But now everything she wore was ripped and what skin Hama could see through the holes was in advanced stages of frostbite.

"I'm sorry," he said quickly, with honest regret and

not a small bit of shock. But she was beyond listening. She was huddled in the corner, her knees up to her chin, her shivering arms around her calves. She was looking right through him, her eyes wild, her mouth working, some strange noises emerging.

Hama went to her slowly, his expression one of sincere concern. He kneeled a few feet away from her, unsure that she was even aware he was there. He carefully held out his left hand to her, trying to gauge the extent of her wounds. She did not bolt, but she stopped shivering and stared intently at the approaching hand.

She let it touch her. When she found it was warm, or relatively so, she even yielded to it. She closed her eyes and cooed. She rubbed herself against Hama's palm like a housecat that wanted attention. Hama took the time to examine her carefully. His eyes finally concentrated on the intimacy she exposed by having her knees at her chin. He could see the area between her legs was uncovered and bloody.

The girl had been sexually molested repeatedly.

A certain amount of understanding flooded his brain. He now knew fairly well why he was sent here. What he was going to do about it was fairly clear as well. *How* he was going to do it was still a bit beyond him.

He snapped out of his tangent when he felt the girl stiffen. She was staring in wide-eyed horror at the ice-filled stake he still held in his right hand.

"No!" she managed to moan. "You must... you must return this...!" she grunted as her hands reached achingly for the spike. He allowed her to wrest it from him. But he quickly took it back as she crawled toward the temple's entrance.

"No, I'll do it," he promised.

She collapsed on her side, at first panic-stricken, then relaxing when she focused her eyes on him. She raised one hand weakly and rubbed his bald head. "Priest," she murmured, "you'll do . . . what's right."

Hama agreed and went outside. He looked again at the bleak surroundings, then threw the stake away. He quickly returned to the girl's side.

"Is it . . .?" she asked anxiously, trying to get up.

"Yes," he said, soothing her, taking her cold body in his arms. He sat with her stretched across his lap, feeling bottomless sorrow. "It has been returned to its proper place." She relaxed in his grip, almost becoming slack. "What has happened here? Who has done this to you?"

"It's all right," she whispered. "You're here now. All the others are dead. All Buddha's soldiers . . . but you're here now."

She sighed, the exhalation ending in the same sort of rattle the wind had. He felt her spirit leaving her shell behind. He felt the essentially imperceptible change in weight as she died in his arms. He laid her on the temple floor and retrieved his stick. He looked down at her prone body on its back. The eyes were still open but they were no longer haunted. Her expression was peaceful—the kind of peace only a reprieve from Hell can create.

*   *   *

Hama slammed back the door of the inn, the wind whipping the snow around him and across the threshold. Those half-dozen huddled inside started at the intrusion as if they were expecting a maddened, crimson tengu to cut them all down. But then they recognized the robes and bald head of the monk.

"Buddha be praised!" a man exclaimed, running forward. "Come in, priest, quickly!" An old woman to the left started crying on her companion's shoulder, saying something about how she couldn't believe the deities could hear their prayers all the way out here and how she had given up all hope.

Hama slammed the door of the inn behind him. He had searched for so long to find it. All the houses he had come upon since leaving the temple were as deserted as the wharf-front shacks. The occupants had obviously fled to some sort of fortress, and this looked like it. Now he was faced by three anxious men, all crowding him near the front door.

"You have heard of our troubles?" one asked.

"You have come to help us?" said another.

Theirs were ruddy, desperate faces. The island people were a hardy lot, but hardly equipped for violence. The peasant tradition of collapsing and whining in the face of trouble had not lessened here. After several hundred years beneath the heels of the samurai, it was little wonder. The peasant farmers and fishermen had been taught for generations to be fourth-class citizens.

Hama brusquely moved around them, heading toward the boiling pot of water over the interior fire, which took up most of the inn's center. He warmed his hands, then turned, lifting his robe's tail, so his rear could be thawed. "I've heard nothing," he growled. "But I haven't liked what I've seen!"

"What?" the man who had initially greeted him pressed. "What have you seen?"

"Discarded prayer tablets. Religious statues that have been disfigured. Hollowed-out stakes filled with water, positioned around a gravesite. A human bone in a tree. A skeleton sitting in its branches..." The woman who had been babbling suddenly cried out and started wailing in earnest. Hama shouted over her noise.

"A sexually molested girl cowering behind a temple altar! Deserted homes. Abandoned boats. People huddled in cowering fear inside an inn!"

The men just stared bug-eyed at him. "Tell me!" Hama demanded, stamping his numb feet. "Say it! He will always have you in his power if you can not even say it!"

The men's mouths worked.

"Vampire," one whispered.

2

Vampire.

All the signs had been there, especially the bones in the tree. The Japanese believed that the vampire stole souls, not drank blood. The drinking blood idea came from a European exploiting the legends that started in the Orient. Those legends were not of Romanian impalers or long-toothed bloodsuckers, they were of pathetic humans who had died. Instead of becoming spirits or ghosts, they became horrid creatures who could change themselves into trees—of all things.

The arms of these trees could snare unwary passersby—sucking out their souls and ingesting their bodies until only the bleached white bones were left. The solution? Tradition dictated that the villagers search out the vampire once they discovered bones in a tree. The

monster lived in its grave, and was usually the latest to
have died in the village.

Wooden stakes were hollowed out and driven into
the ground on all four corners of the gravesite. Then
purifying water was poured into the spikes' holes. That
ancient cure obviously did not work here in Ogami.
The hacked shrines were evidence of that. When faith
did not work, the hysterical creations often turned on
their makers.

"Tell me," Hama demanded of them.

"Warui!" another woman comforting the babbling
woman suddenly cried. *"Dame!"* "Bad, evil, you mustn't
speak of it!"

"But this is a soldier of Buddha, Hiroki," one of the
men said, going to her and motioning toward the monk.

"So were the others!" she retorted stridently. "Did it
save them?"

"What?" Hama interrupted, looking to the two men
who still stood by him.

"The others," the innkeeper said cautiously. "At the
temple—"

"Do not tell him!" the woman flared. They all stared
at him—in amazement, in shame, in fear. She sat
straight, staring at Hama defiantly. "I am sorry. I no
longer believe in Buddha." Some gasped. Even the
babbling wailer quieted. "Look at our beautiful town,"
she said, arms out.

The yamabushi stepped forward and hit her across
the face with his open palm. The blow sent her to the
floor as if the Lord had struck her down. She shot out of
her seat and hit the wood planks heavily.

The man who had spoken to the woman rushed to her side. Hama grabbed the layers of cloth that covered the man's shoulders and hurled him back as if throwing a rodent off a cake. The man left the ground, slammed down on his shoulders and slid into the heated bath near the rear of the room.

The other men moved as if to aid him but stopped when Hama threw his arms wide, blocking their path. "I will not hear this talk," he said vehemently. "Do not disgrace yourselves or the dead."

His violence had its desired effect. First, he established himself as the leader, and second, he had convinced them that he was a worthy adversary of this evil. The others stared at him in surprised reverence. It was obvious from their faces that this was the first time they had felt hope in a long while. He soon got the entire story.

The vampire had come to Ogami some months back. At first it seemed content to kill occasionally. After completing a ritual around the gravesite of one Taki Mashimuri, they thought they had the problem solved— only then, the vampire seemed to delight in taunting them by beginning a program of terror.

Victims would disappear, some never to return. Others would be found unspeakably tortured—as if the vampiric process had not been completed. Their flayed bones—hunks of flesh and muscle still clinging to their rended bodies—would be discovered. Other victims were found in scattered pieces, forcing the populace to wait for all the bones to be collected before they could attempt to identify the corpse.

And still others were returned alive—but they were too weak, wounded, or insane to stay alive long. In some cases the torture was psychological—the vampire had literally scared his victim to death. In the temple girl's case, the torture had obviously been sexual. She had taken refuge at the altar after all the area priests had been systematically eradicated. In fact, they were among the first to go.

The town had practically gone crazy. All the Buddhist monks had been exterminated by the vampire. The single police officer and military representative had been killed. No one ever answered their many messages. Hama could imagine why. All lines of communication were probably cut. All the fleet-footed messengers who had been sent probably lay dead somewhere.

Finally the town had turned in on itself. Neighbor started accusing neighbor. Neighbor started killing neighbor. Any one who could possibly have been the vampire was attacked. All the graves had been dug up and the corpses burned. The ashes had been thrown into the sea. The deities had been disfigured in the people's helpless rage—after orgies of praying proved useless.

Until these six remained. Hama discovered each one's identity. Ultimately, their names and histories were irrelevant, useless. After their experiences, they too turned out to be useless.

"Go to the temple," Hama instructed. "There is a dead girl there. Give her a proper burial."

They stiffened. Hama looked at them all. The men's eyes practically bugged out. The women's eyelids suddenly seemed to get very heavy.

"Do as I say," Hama told them solemnly.

No one moved. "She may be the one," a man whispered.

"*Baka!*" Hama exploded. Fool. "She has been raped repeatedly. She suffered a terrible death."

"The mark of the vampire!" a woman said decisively.

Hama silenced them all with a look. "No wonder this fate has befallen you," he said. "You are fish in a net, badgers caught in metal traps, then slaughtered." He shook his head in disgust. "Do as I say!" he suddenly shouted. They all looked at him intently. "You too will die unless you do as I say. Go to the temple and perform the rites. Only then might you redeem your souls. In this condition the monster can reach you from afar."

The logic of it gripped them. Their souls were indeed diseased. Might it then make sense that the vampire could capture their beings without even touching them . . . ?

"Go," said Hama. "I must hurry." He walked with them to the road and then went his separate way. Going with them would serve no purpose. Besides, they disgusted him. Sheep, lemmings, weasels. No wonder the samurai had often cut them down in decades past, seemingly without provocation. Their pathetic inferior demeanor invited nothing but disdain.

Hama quickly strode down the frozen road, letting the biting air clear the stench from his mind and nostrils. He marched right to the nearest house and pushed the front door open. These were not the fine homes of the mainland, with their elegantly simple sliding door systems. These were crude homes with swinging wood doors—better to keep the seawind out, once closed.

Inside was a simple room: a sleeping area near the now cold fire and a table in the center of the floor. Hama placed his staff on the tabletop and pulled off the wrapped cloth from over his shoulder. Lifting his robe, he wrapped the material around his torso. When finished, he was wearing his thick beige robe on the outside with no hint of color adorning it.

When Hama returned to the road, his vestments seemed to blend with the wind and drifting snow. He walked unerringly back toward the waterfront. He carefully searched each shack there, until he was certain each was empty and held no clue to the vampire's location. The only thing he gained from the time-consuming trip was an oar.

He used that to good purpose by finding the least corroded boat and jumping in. Untying it from the dock, he set off for the coast of Haboro. Hama practically sang as he stood on the back of the skiff and guided it across the choppy waves, through the treacherous wind. His muscles did not whine the way the air around him did. Instead he exalted in the way his flesh ignored the cold and his body ignored the effort it took to get the craft across the frosty water.

He had never felt this magnificent, this certain. It was a combination of self-fulfillment and a feeling of power over the peons he had just left. He knew what his life meant now—he had been made aware of his purpose in the strange world he had been born into . . . twice.

He reached the Haboro shore in less time than it had taken the professional boatman to get him there. That boatman himself was his only witness. In weather such as this, on a day such as this, only the hardiest—or foolhardiest—man would be plying his trade.

The boatman approached to help Hama tie up his boat. "Find anyone?" the boatman asked.

"You knew," Hama said, looking at the man's profile.

"Of course," said the boatman, eyes on the skiff. "Didn't you?"

"No," Hama admitted, as the boatman straightened. "I knew nothing of what was happening in Ogami until I arrived there earlier today."

"I'm sorry, priest," the boatman said humbly. "If I had known I would have warned you."

Hama waited until he bowed slightly in apology before trying to kill him.

He swung his stick up and his hand out at the same time. The boatman seemed to slide back and roll off to the right at the same time. Hama's hand, which had shot forward as if extending the palm in greeting, did not even touch the target: the boatman's collarbone.

The stick did not reach its destination either. As soon as the man had moved, Hama stopped its swing and tried to catch the boatman in his side with the tip. The boatman grabbed the end as he stood on the edge of the dock, and the two faced each other across the six-foot stick. The boatman was hunched over, grinning. Hama stood with his feet wide, anchored in position.

"Ironic," Hama declared. "You hoped either I or the survivors would complete your task." In other words, the "vampire" hoped the townspeople would have attacked Hama, he killing them or they killing him.

A survivor had told Hama that no SOS, no message for help had been answered. What was the best way to ensure this? Kill the messengers. On an island, the best way to get every messenger was to be the boatman who brought them across the bay. And, as a boatman, he could see anyone coming who wasn't in his boat. And since they were fighting a "vampire," they never suspected him.

He would wait until night, when no Haboro or Ogami fisherman would brave the treacherous waters, then brave the treacherous water himself . . . to claim more victims.

As the boatman and yamabushi spoke and watched one another, seemingly motionless, a titanic struggle was going on. They were testing each other's strength on either end of the stick. They exerted pressure, pushing and pulling, trying to throw each other off balance. But the stick never moved.

Suddenly Hama swung the end he was holding up, forcing the other end down. He grabbed the stick in both hands and pushed. The boatman instantly let go. Hama tried to smash the point into both the boatman's feet, but the man danced away, moving each leg as Hama drove the stick end back and forth.

Hama swung the staff up, trying to catch the boatman between the legs. The man dove backward in a somersault. The stick missed him. Hama brought it back, and forward again, trying to splash the man's features across his skull as he became upright. But the head suddenly seemed to rest on ball bearings instead of a neck. The skull swung this way and that, wherever the staff tip wasn't.

The man kept dodging and Hama kept thrusting as both ran down the wharf—the boatman running backward. He held his ground at the very edge of the dock. Hama pulled the stick back and rammed it at the boatman's midsection. The boatman swiveled, the stick missing him. Hama tried again, with the same result.

Hama stopped and stepped back, bringing the stick beside him in a defiant posture. The boatman just stood there, legs wide, on the very edge of the wharf.

The yamabushi didn't like it. He hated it, in fact. The man could have grabbed the stick at any time and fought Hama back to more secure footing, but he didn't. He was that sure of himself. The two men faced each other again; their faces reflecting the exact same emotions as before: the yamabushi, grimness; the boatman, amusement.

They stood like that in the driving wind and sleet for what seemed to be a very long time . . . until the horizon began to darken over the men's shoulders. Night was coming, bringing with it somber colors that painted the sky in purples and dark reds. In this light, the insane murderer was almost . . . poetic.

There was the difference, you see. Hama had known no one but murderers. His father was a murderer, his mother was a murderer, his teachers were murderers. But they were not insane. They murdered for a reason, maybe even for a cause. Not this man. He was a beast gone wild. A beast who had to be put down.

"I have been waiting for you," said the man, though his lips hardly moved. The words just seemed to come to Hama's ears of their own accord. "I have been waiting to see what they could possibly send to kill me." Pause. "And I must admit the old *dobutsus* have once again been able to surprise me." A chuckle. "Just when I thought no one could."

"You dare call *them* animals?" Hama flared. "After what you have done?"

"I expect an executioner and they send me a child." All mirth fled from the boatman's voice and features. "You don't have the proper attitude for this, *kodomo*," he scolded the child. "Let's see if you have the skills."

Hama brought the stick down at the boatman's head almost faster than the eye could see. Almost.

The boatman disappeared.

The wood beneath his feet splintered and he fell through to the water so quickly, it appeared he had simply vanished. But Hama knew better. He let the pole's swing carry him forward. He leaped off the wharf edge as he heard the splash. He landed in his skiff and brought the pole down into the displaced water the diving boatman had left.

The wood touched nothing but liquid. Hama stood in the boat, waiting for any sign of the man's position. His eyes had to be everywhere, his ears had to hear everything. He stood, seemingly serene and still, waiting for a ripple, a bubble, a wave, anything.

The skiff exploded from the water, the boatman beneath it, lifting it as he would a weighted bar. Hama leaped up and dove over. He slammed into one of the wharf's uprights and held on as if hugging a lover. His right arm swung back—the staff in it driving the attacking boatman away.

The man dove again. Hama scrambled up the ice-laden timber to the wharf. He raced diagonally across it and jumped again, landing on the beach. He immediately raced to a system of nets hung on oars. He pulled two oars out of the ground and threw them like spears. Each slammed into a boat tied to the wharf. Both splintered the bottom of the crafts. They started to sink immediately. So much for the boatman escaping that way.

Hama could take no chances, although he soon learned the man had no intention of escaping. He stood on the shore, waiting, again using all his skills, but when the man appeared, it was without warning. Nothing spectacular, he merely emerged from the sea. But that was enough to concern Hama. He had only noticed the boatman the moment his head emerged from the waves. A yamabushi should . . . *had* to do better.

The boatman stood on the shore across from Hama, drenched. "You are not ready," he said, reading the younger man's mind. Hama gave no hint of his doubts.

"But I am here."

"You will die."

"What difference does that make? To me?"

The boatman was impressed. He looked to the sand and chuckled. "Or to me?"

"You know why I am here, renegade," Hama said softly.

The boatman looked up then. Again he shook his head. "You don't have the right attitude," he repeated. "You are too haughty. Too certain."

"I *am* certain," Hama agreed. "How could any man see what you have done and not be certain?"

"Because any man would seek to discover *why*."

Hama made a face. "Irrelevant."

"No!" the boatman said. It was the first word he had expended any real emotion on. "If you knew why, none of this would have happened!"

Hama scoffed again, his meaning clear. Knowing why wouldn't bring any of the victims back. It was a classic murderer's attitude. It seemed to be just what the boatman wanted. He responded to it. Hama was just as glad to let him rave. He dreaded the final confrontation. In the back of his mind, he was uncertain he could accomplish his goal.

"You know what it is like," the boatman said almost pleadingly.

"They teach you to kill," Hama prompted.

"Yes!" he agreed, his teeth clenched. Clenched to prevent their chattering. He had survived his icy plunge, but emerging from the freezing water to the freezing air was taking its toll . . . even on such as he.

"You lose the purpose," Hama concluded derisively.

"No! Don't you see? The purpose is to kill. So I kill." He swept his arm toward the island of Ogami. It all seemed crystal-clear to him. His face lit up as if he had delivered unarguable logic.

"Not them," Hama said pedantically. "You are told who to kill."

The boatman looked as if this hadn't occurred to him. "My purpose is to kill," he repeated. "That was what I was trained for. What I was taught to do from the very instant of my birth." He seemed to be trying to find the end of his logic so he could grab on and swing to safety.

"That is my *entire* purpose," he said suddenly. "I have no past, no future. I have given it all up for this. For the killing I live. For the killing I die. There is nothing else. No previous life, no afterlife."

"By choosing this way, you have rejected any other way," Hama agreed.

"I didn't . . ." the boatman began, then let confusion overwhelm him. Admitting that he had no choice in the matter was beyond his ability. He had been born into the family. The choice had been made for him. He could not argue in the face of that.

"You are ninja," Hama said. "No life on earth, no life in heaven."

The boatman stared at Hama, unsure, angry.

"You have rejected even that," Hama continued. "You have betrayed your family, threatened their security."

The boatman looked as if he couldn't believe that he was the one Hama was talking about. Put into words, it was totally unbelievable. Betrayed the family? Threatened the security? Impossible.

"Family first, then country," the boatman said to himself. "The samurai had to follow the Emperor first, then family. They had to hire us to solve problems when family was threatened by family. Family within the family. Had to protect family but could not hurt family. Had to... had to... use us."

"That time is over," Hama reminded him. "That era ended fifty years ago."

"But the war..." the boatman complained. "We will lose the war."

He saw the twisted, tortured souls. He saw them dancing in Hades. All the heavens were Hades.

The time had come. The logic had caught up with itself. It would chomp upon its own tail any second.

"You have betrayed your family. Threatened their security," Hama repeated. "Do as you must," he demanded.

The boatman stood, his head down, his arms at his side. The sleeves were shaking slightly.

"Do as you must before I..." Hama repeated.

"What difference will it make?" the boatman asked the sky in anguish. "My soul can never rest in peace. I have no soul."

"You have honor! Your family has honor!"

The boatman looked up, directly at Hama. For a second the words seemed to reach him. Then suddenly he smiled again. His expression became mirthful, sardonic. He wagged a finger at the priest. "Oh, no. Not after this."

"You can still make it right!" Hama promised.

"Oh, no. Not with you here... my dear executioner. You are here, so it is already too late."

He had been born, raised, and trained to kill, but he had lost direction to think his only purpose was to kill. He had run from his alternately nurturing and torturing

family to this island. He had made the residents think a
vampire had cursed them, then killed them one by one
until only six were left. He killed, waiting—probably
hoping—for his executioner, the yamabushi, to come.
There had been plenty of time for seppuku before.

But now, with the warrior-priest here, he had to die
by the executioner's hand . . . or he was not worthy of
death at all.

He walked toward Hama.

Hama ran away.

The ninja was surprised. He did not know that Hama
was running out of pure, depthless fear, and not some
sort of clever strategy. Hama knew, behind the gauze of
fright, that the maneuver was ridiculous, but he didn't
know what else to do.

They caught up to each other on the path leading to
the Haboro road. Hama felt the ninja's presence and
whirled around, a fist, a leg, and the staff swinging. The
ninja had to dive back to avoid all three. Hama hurled
the stick. It bounced off the ninja's chest; not injuring
him, but touching him, actually touching him!

The ninja swung his arm into the stick, spinning it
around. Hama grabbed the other end. It looked to both
as if the ninja had thrown the weapon back into Hama's
grasp. He moved forward to take advantage of the lucky
blow, twisting the stick in and forward.

The ninja grabbed the free end and brought his fist
down on the stick a third up its length. The branch
broke under the blow. Hama fell forward, past the
ninja. He somersaulted just over the ground and spun
the remainder of the stick at the man's ankles. The

ninja somersaulted over the stick, landing a few feet from the path.

Hama dove toward the road. The ninja leaped to cut him off. Hama raced in the other direction. The ninja went after him. Hama suddenly stopped and kicked backward. The ninja swung his right forearm to knock the leg aside, still moving forward. He slammed his other fist into Hama's midriff.

Hama slid back, the wrapped cloth around his middle protecting his ribs but not dissipating the pain completely. He cartwheeled twice to gain more distance from the ninja and recover. But when he became upright again, the ninja was right there. Hama swung the stick again, but the ninja knocked it from the yamabushi's hand.

Hama blocked the following blows frantically. They traded fists, legs, and feet, each blocking each other's attacks expertly. They disengaged for a second, then met each other again. Their patterns of attack were violent and rudimentary. They plumbed each other's knowledge of karate and judo. Each sought attacks and holds as the other blocked and escaped.

To Hama's eyes, the ninja had become his father. The hands and feet that came at him were his father's. Lo and behold, the battle was no longer frightening. He could match his father, because his father was trying to train him, not kill him. Oh, sure, his father would be willing to hurt him. But only Hama's own stupidity would let his father kill him.

The ninja kicked at Hama's head. He blocked, twisted, and pushed. He swept his own leg around, tripping the ninja. He grabbed the ninja's calf and pushed the man to the road. The ninja twisted out of Hama's grip and started to get up. Hama pounded at him with both fists. The blows connected but didn't find their marks.

The ninja pushed Hama away and started his leg attack again. Hama deflected the blows but couldn't get any of his own licks in. He watched the torrent of kicks for any sign of an opening. That was a mistake. He took his eyes off the ninja's arms. He never saw them move. He only saw the shuriken that sped through the ninja's kicks.

The four-bladed throwing star that the ninja had taken from his waistband thudded into Hama's waist. The yamabushi spun around, his arms flailing. He slammed to the road face first, atop his broken stick. Snow seemed to bounce around him. He shuddered, convulsed, then lay still.

The ninja stepped back for balance, then surveyed the fallen figure. It was that simple, was it? Not easy, but simple. What would happen now? Would they send another yamabushi for him? then another, and another? He couldn't think about that now. First he had to find shelter. He shivered, clamping his teeth together again, but unable to keep them from chattering.

He moved toward Hama, who tried to shatter his kneecap and break his leg.

But all Hama's kick did was push the ninja back. He was not good enough to gather the energy for a leg-breaking blow from a still, prone position. The ninja was surprised, however. He had not seen any evidence of Hama's survival. So when the kick came, it knocked

him to his back. He prepared himself to defend against
his own shuriken.

But Hama was not that foolish. He would not put the
throwing star back into the ninja's hands, in case he
missed. While he was prone, he thought of something
better. He rose, the small bag of rice on his rope belt
pouring out white kernels. That had been the "bouncing snow." The shuriken had hit the rice bag, slowed
just enough not to penetrate the layers of cloth Hama
had wrapped around his middle.

The ninja cursed himself for not throwing it harder,
but he had wanted to kill his executioner with finesse.
He had wanted to watch the man die of the poisoned
blades after having thrown it just hard enough to break
the yamabushi's skin. Now he watched Hama rise instead, the blade embedded in the end of his stick.

The staff had become a tomahawk, which Hama
swung and jabbed at the ninja as he slid down the
street on his back. The ninja "walked" with his shoulders, hips and legs, keeping his torso out of range of the
new, makeshift, weapon, and kicking whatever blows
came near his feet. He suddenly anchored himself,
kicked another shuriken-chop away and pushed himself
off the ground, toward Hama.

He rammed his toes into Hama's solar plexus, then
dropped back. He somersaulted over his own shoulders
and got to his feet before Hama was able to move
forward again. The next attack they both met standing.
The ninja came forward, seemingly fearless of the stick
and shuriken. He drove Hama back, his attack brutally
certain. He seemed angry, almost desperate.

Hama kept the image of his father in his mind. He could lose to this ninja. He didn't dare lose to his father.

It was not enough. The ninja's battering was flowing, defined, and brilliant. He took advantage of Hama's situation. He didn't seem to see the weapon as a problem; he saw it as an advantage. It kept one of Hama's fists filled. He attacked Hama's body and the weapon arm: blocking, battering, blocking again, slamming Hama's chest again. And each block was actually a blow. He was hitting Hama's arms with his own arms each time. Not just protecting himself, but attacking.

And suddenly the ninja's feet were in the contest. Block, blow, crouch, kick. By then, even the crouch was an attack, his feet snaking behind Hama's legs to trip him.

At first, Hama was able to defend himself. But that was all he was doing. He was not fighting back. Then some punches began getting through, battering his middle. Finally, he was completely in the ninja's control. As fast as he could move backward, the ninja matched him. As quickly as he spun the weapon and his fist around, the ninja could stop it.

He could only use his legs for attempted escape, not for fighting. His arms seemed like so many marionette limbs. The shuriken-stick seemed to be a candy cane. The ninja hit him again and again. There were no more blocks. Each was a strike: back of fist to arm, knuckles to solar plexus, foot to calf, arm to wrist, fist to face, foot to stomach.

Finally he struck knuckles to fingers, and the shuriken-stick fell from Hama's numb hand. His fist struck the other arm, knocking it wide, exposing Hama's entire torso and face. The side of his foot connected with jaw, lifting Hama's feet from the ground. He collapsed onto the road flat on his back.

When his eyes cleared, he saw the ninja crouched above him. The man's eyes were glassy, his expression set. His right arm was cocked back, his middle knuckle extended to drive into Hama's throat or between his eyes or into his temple—the killing blow.

Hama experienced nothing: no life blasting past his eyes, no words in his mind. He simply lay, frozen, waiting for a death which never came.

The yamabushi lay there and the ninja crouched for several seconds before anything happened. Then the latter collapsed dead from exposure.

3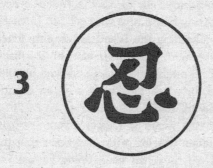

Hama did not know how long he had been helpless. He had not seen the ninja struggle to remain upright after defeating him. He had not seen the ninja stumble. He had not seen the ninja shake uncontrollably. All he saw was the ninja kneeling alongside him. And even then he was not certain what he had seen. A man dead in a killing position? A man dying on one knee, his eyes open, his arm back?

As he walked slowly south, toward Nemuri, Hama initially doubted everything he had seen. An island gripped in fear of a vampire? Everyone on the island dead, except a half-dozen people? A skeleton smiling down from a tree? What had the ninja been doing there?

Hama pictured the boatman ripping flesh, muscle, and sinew from a victim's limbs in the glow of moonlight. He saw him bleaching the bones. He saw him raping, murdering, skinning, and gutting his victims. All with an all-too-earthly gleam in his eye.

All a dream. It must have been. It must be. All a dream of contorting souls across the Japanese sky.

Six Allied Army battleships were off Iwo Jima. Planes had been bombarding the island for seventy-four days straight. Lieutenant General Tadamichi Kuribayashi's men had built tunnels, laid minefields, and manned six hundred and forty-two blockhouses on an island that was essentially all shore.

And up on the island of Ogami a vampire had just died. A mountain-warrior priest had been sent to execute a ninja—as they had been doing for a thousand years.

Hama made his way home with a gift for his teachers. He had it under his arm the entire trip. He had it on the table while he was eating in inns along the way. He never let it out of his sight. He even slept with it. With winter at its worst, with temperatures below freezing, with the sky almost always gray, he returned to the Nemuri temple with his special gift.

It was midafternoon when he arrived. He entered through the forest, with every tree looking like clutching fingers reaching for a clear, shining heaven. The snow clung to the trunks like blankets of white blood. The ice hung from the branch tips like frozen tears.

The graceful arch of the temple roof held no pleasure for Hama's eyes. Nor did the appearance of his three teachers in the entrance. Exhaustion covered him like his robes. The cold was in his joints like crystalline marrow. Every move brought stabbing pain in his limbs and a dull, pounding pain in his head.

Hama somberly fell to his knees in the snow before them as they stood on the clean wood of the temple's porch floor. Silently he held his package up to them. With a motion, the center teacher instructed him to show them. Hama unwrapped the ninja's head and held it out to them by the hair.

The teacher to his left took it from him and looked into its shrunken, rolled-up eyes. Then he quietly took it inside the temple. Hama remained on his knees, his head down. He looked into the snow, trying to find some sort of sign, any sort of heavenly signal on how he should proceed. He had a secret and his heart was black. But all he saw was the line of the rich wood floor and the roughness of the muddy white ground. Maybe that was all the sign he deserved.

He only looked up after the third teacher returned. For a fourth set of feet had joined the trio. He raised his head to stare into the face of his father.

He could not recall ever feeling such emotion. So much hate. He couldn't believe his body could hold so much hate. A hate that threatened to tear him open, to rip his skin from his fingernails and toenails, to come pouring from every orifice.

The hate overwhelmed everything else. It overwhelmed the fear. The fear of not being able to understand why he hated his father so. It overwhelmed the love. The love he felt for his home and his family. The blade edge of his emotion cut directly across the feelings, separating the love and hate by a hair's length.

But the hate was too powerful. It swept over the fear and love in a rolling, bright-blue wave. It crested in frothy white and crashed down on everything else, blinding him to his father's proud, concerned face.

"You have succeeded in all we have asked you to do," a teacher finally said. It was the teacher to the left—a small man with wisps of long gray hair coming from his scalp, his lip, and his chin. "You have survived your ordeal and your test. Do you know what you are and what you are to do?"

"Yes, teacher," Hama said quietly, looking to the ground again. His hands were on his knees. His knees were soaked through with mud and snow.

"No, I am not your teacher," the old man corrected.

Hama looked up at the others. "Teachers?" he inquired of the others, his voice far away, forlorn. They simply turned and walked away, disappearing inside the temple.

"You have no more teachers," the old man said. "They can no longer speak with you." Hama looked at the man to his right, the little one who was speaking. His face expressed sorrow. "You have no need of them anymore. You need no more teachers. Only 'Hanshi.'"

Hama's father stepped down from the temple porch and sat on his knees in the snow beside his son. *"Hanshi minna imasu,"* he said. *"Hanshi zenbu imasu. Kessh'te wasuremasu."*

The old man smiled and nodded at the father. Hama's father took his sword—the straight sword—from his belt and held it up to the Hanshi with both hands, his head down. The Hanshi took it.

"Hama," he said, using the name that had come to the fourteen-year-old boy in his burial delirium. The eighteen-year-old looked up as ordered. Every word, no matter how expressed, had been an order since the day he could understand. The Hanshi presented the sword to him. Hama looked to his father. The man's expression became enraged.

"Hanshi minna imasu!" he angrily hissed. He was saying that he was nothing before the Hanshi. To look at him for approval was sacrilege.

Hama took the sword, resting it on his knees and bowing low. The Hanshi nodded sagely.

"Up," the father announced, rising sharply to his feet. Hama learned his lesson quickly. He looked to the Hanshi for approval this time. The Hanshi nodded. Hama rose to face his father, his father's scabbarded sword in his hand. As far as he was concerned, that should have been it. The young man had succeeded in his challenges, and the responsibilities had been passed from father to son. But that was not all, as it turned out. His father charged him.

Hama held the sword away, sparring with his father almost casually, thinking the final part of this ritual was proving his skill to the Hanshi. His father fought him with energy at first, but when he sensed the boy's apathy, he attacked with aggression. He kicked his son in the side and threw the back of his fist across Hama's mouth.

Hama spun away, his lips split. He turned once and stopped, gingerly touching his mouth. His fingertips came away wet and red. Throwing the blood to the white ground, Hama looked around for someplace to put the sword. He saw the Hanshi shaking his head.

All right, old man, Hama thought. Be that way. He charged across the temple grounds, the sword held midway down its sheathed length. At the last second before getting in range of his father, he switched it to his left hand, automatically distracting his father's eyes, and let him have a rapid flurry of kicks and right-hand punches.

His father just managed to deflect the assault but had to keep moving back, his feet dragging in the snow. He seemed destined to back into a tree, then suddenly moved forward again, taking the initiative. He peppered his renewed attack with roundhouse kicks and vicious side thrusts.

Hama kept moving back but irritably knocked each foot thrust aside with the tip of the sword scabbard. His father finally tried a punch. Hama moved in, pivoting, jamming the sword along his father's front—the hilt under his chin and along his jawline. With a sudden sharp twist and pull of both arms, Hama flipped his father over. The man landed on his back.

Hama straightened, feeling satisfaction at last. The throw had been completely successful. His father landed hard. So hard that he slid for several feet in the snow. Hama relaxed, thinking the show of skill was over and he could finally get some rest. He was fed up with the whole thing. But his father only sprang to his feet and ran back toward him.

Hama raised his hands and turned his head aside as if to say "That's enough," but all he got in reply was his father's fist against his ear. The blow staggered him, nearly knocking him over. But before he could slip, Hama snarled and yanked the sword from its sheath. He swung it before him in an arc, meaning to send his father back.

But the man did not retreat. To Hama's surprise, he attempted to move forward. Instead, Hama stepped back in confusion and jabbed the sword at his father's stomach again. To Hama's astonishment, the man almost rammed his stomach on the blade tip. If Hama had not yanked the sword back, it would have pierced him.

Hama retreated, his eyes and mouth moving. The Hanshi merely looked on, his beneficent expression frozen. Hama's father's face was pinched and concentrated on the sword. Hama looked to the blade, then shook his head, mouthing the word, *"lie."* No. He turned and began to walk rapidly away.

His father raced after him. He kicked Hama in the back. Hama stumbled forward, then began to run through the trees. His father ran around them to cut him off with a battery of savage kicks. Hama danced back, using the trees as his limbs, blocking his father's effectiveness. He moved back the way he had come, hoping to escape around the side of the temple.

A shadow passed over him and he felt a displacement above him. He automatically brought the sword up. It snagged something. He felt liquid across his back and neck.

He jerked the sword down and felt at the nape of his neck. A new red smear was on his fingertips. He looked up as his father landed before him, his left leg cut along the side from his knee to his hip. His kimono was sliced open and blood streamed down his pant leg.

He nearly collapsed, but not quite. Instead he clumsily found his balance and jabbed a fist at Hama's face. Hama saw it coming as if in slow motion. He fully meant to let the coarsened, permanently swollen knuckles smash him in the face. He let them come at him, his mouth open, his eyes wide. Not until the fist blotted out everything in his vision, including his father's face, did he instinctively react.

Again the sword came up. He held it before his own face, his nose touching the rear of the blade. His father's fist hit the blade edge—cutting the hand open between the second and third knuckle.

Hama sucked in his breath. He reared back in horror as blood spit across his face. He swung the sword behind him, just so he would not use it again. He could not bring himself to throw it away. Everything in his being demanded that he not throw it away. It would be the same as throwing himself away. And if he had wanted to do that, he would have told them how the ninja had actually died.

Hama kept the sword behind him so he would not swing it before him to keep his father away. Because it would not keep his father away. His father would move right into the blade's path.

Hama tried to bring himself to run from the temple courtyard. But he could not do that, either. He had returned simply to be here, to show he understood. He was yamabushi now. He had killed his first renegade ninja, as his people had done for hundreds of years.

There had to be an executioner for the ninjas who could not live under the strain of their existence. There had to be someone other than the ninjas themselves to put the miserable monsters out of their misery. The ninjas themselves might let the maniac kill indiscriminately for their own insidious purposes. The ninjas were murderers outside society, anyway. They needed an executioner outside the society as well.

Riddle: what do you use to kill a monster?

Answer: another monster, of course.

Hama moved around the courtyard. His father shambled after him, blood pouring from his wounds. Hama went to the Hanshi, hoping he could ask for some sort of clemency without shaming everything. But as he approached, he glanced back and saw his father's infuriated, anguished face. To near the Hanshi with a drawn sword was unforgivable.

But there was something else on his face as well. A rage. The rage that had driven him all these years. He was angry at his son for "ruining" things. Everything the father had done for the son was leading up to this moment. And now the idiot boy was going to throw it away?

Hama stopped. He did not look at the Hanshi. He stood hunched over and grinning, until he realized he looked exactly as the boatman had.

He straightened and swung the sword to either side, his breath escaping his lips in two jagged snorts. The thin, short trees to either side of him were cut in half, their frail branches falling to the ground.

It did not even slow his father. The man came forward, his cleaved hand held up and his sliced leg dragging. He shambled toward his son like a monster.

Hama held the sword out, smiling. He pointed the tip at his father's chest.

Let's see him do it, he thought.

His father did it. He ran forward as fast as he could and jumped on the sword tip. He pushed himself along the blade, the point between his chest and stomach. It went in directly under the sternum bone.

Hama held it tightly, his mind blank. He watched his father force himself deeper and deeper along the sword as if watching a Noh theater performance. How melodramatic, how predictable.

He felt the sword go through organs. He saw blood burble up around the edges of the hole in his father's torso. He saw the blood spurt up the bright silver blade.

His father's arms reached forward, his fingers clutching the air. His eyelids closed and opened repeatedly. There was white flesh outlining his nose and mouth. His face looked like a mask.

His fingers clamped onto his son's upper arms. Using them as leverage, he pulled himself all the way onto the blade. The point came out his back and kept going.

His face came at Hama. The . . . thing wearing the human mask of his father's face just kept coming, until it obliterated everything else. Hama watched the soul writhe in the sky, joining the millions of others.

Finally it moved aside. The world returned to Hama's eyes. His father's chin rested on his shoulder. His father's mouth was next to his ear. He spoke two words and died.

"*Ai Uchi.*"

"Cut him as he cuts you."
"Lack of anger."
"Honor your enemy."
"Abandon your life."
"Throw away fear."

It meant all these things, and more. *Ai Uchi.* The last words from a father to a son. The boy is father to the man. The son becomes the father. There cannot be two fathers. One must step aside for the other.

As the father slowly dropped to the scarlet-splashed snow, Hama had looked at him with empty interest. The patterns...the patterns of crimson in the snow...the way it blended with the white and the brown of the mud.

It didn't look like his father anymore. It was just a shape. An asymmetrical shape. Out of place in this temple of nature's life.

Hama had to pull the sword free. The action rolled his father over. Much to the young man's disgust, his father's eyes were closed. No truly great man died with his eyes closed. A great man died standing up, with his eyes open.

Just as well, Hama thought. His father had not been a great man. He chose to train his son rather than work for his people. He lived only through his son, so it was

only natural he should die by his son. Hama only
wished *he* had killed him, not this automaton who stood
in for him. The automaton turned to the Hanshi, ignoring the human heap beside him.

The Hanshi said nothing. And, at first, he did nothing. He gave no sign. But finally he said, "Go home,"
and returned to the temple interior. It took a great will
of effort for Hama to keep from chopping his father's
head off, then running after the Hanshi and presenting
it to him.

Instead he stood in place for several minutes. Nothing transpired in his face or mind. He might as well
have been buried again. Maybe he was. But soon he
walked away from the body and retrieved the sword's
scabbard. He carefully cleaned the blade in the snow
and returned it to its sheath. Without looking back, he
walked out of the temple courtyard and went home.

On the way he appreciated the logic of it all. It was a
maturation. The young yamabushi had to learn to take
responsibility. He had to learn to accept executions. He
had to do what was best for his people. He had to show
his ability and willingness to do what had to be done.
There were countless reasons for what had transpired in
the temple courtyard. Ultimately, it was a way of showing respect to one's elders and peers. Who better to kill
you but a loved one?

The house was empty, but well tended. Everything
was clean and in its place. It gave Hama's deadened
mind a chance to think about his mother. He didn't hate
her. What was there to hate? He didn't know her. He
only knew the earth. She was just a woman who tended

the house. She took care of it and, occasionally, him—when he showed signs of weakness.

So she was just a woman, like all Japanese women. They served their male masters with their feet bound in the shape of a lotus leaf. They were the same as the peasants—ritualized to the point of nonexistence. No, he didn't hate her. But he didn't love her. He felt nothing for her. Poor, pitiful, stupid woman.

Hama undressed and had a hot bath. He changed into clean clothes for the first time in weeks. He found new monk's clothing laid out in his room. As soon as its crisp sweetness surrounded him, the exhaustion he had been fighting off for days clutched at him.

He lay on his bed mat. Soon he dreamed of the tengu.

The boy was the man. The boy was young, less than ten years of age, but still he was the shaven-headed eighteen-year-old who had returned from Ogami and watched his father pull himself onto the blade of his own sword. It was the man's eyes looking through the head of the young boy. But he saw the young boy too, as others saw him on the narrow Japanese street.

The road was cobbled with dark stones—brown and gray and dark-red ones, stuck all together as if covered in hard chocolate. The tops of the buildings leaned in toward each other as if watching as well. The many people walking back and forth chattered merrily, ignoring the boy. Then suddenly the road was almost empty, then the road was gone.

The street had somehow opened onto a wide, sloping

field. At its crest was a stone embedded in the earth
and a naked whitewood tree. The tree was dying, but it
was not collapsing. It was as strong as if petrified. The
stone was buried, with only its crest poking out of the
brown and green ground. Beyond was pure white,
blue-frosted sky, as if the clouds and the atmosphere
had traded colors.

The boy danced to the tree, laughing. "Look at me!"
he cried. "I am the tengu, I am the tengu!"

He was in the tree, sitting on a high branch, kicking
his feet and laughing. "I am the tengu." And they all
believed him. They came to the tree and worshipped
him. They left plates of food at the tree's base. They
decorated the tree trunk with bright ribbons. They
planted beautiful flowers among the tree's thick roots.
They told each other of their great good fortune, pointing
at the tree with reverence.

The boy ate the food, climbed all over the tree, and
laughed at his own good fortune. He laughed at the silly
people. *He* didn't believe in anything beyond what he
could see and hear and experience. There was nothing
between the blue of the sky and the black of the night.
Nothing lived just over the next hill or behind the
floating clouds. Nothing peeked over the edge of the
horizon. Nothing sparkled inside the rocks and inside
the beads of water.

He laughed at the supernatural. And the supernatural laughed with him. He looked up at the sound. A
tengu was sitting on the next branch up.

The boy gasped, but the tengu's face showed no

malice. He enjoyed a good joke. He liked to laugh at the humans and their strange habits.

"You sure fooled them good!" the tengu declared.

"Yes," the boy said, smiling. "They're silly, aren't they?"

"Silly? Stupid more like."

"Yes, stupid. They're stupid, aren't they?"

"Ridiculous."

"Yes, ridiculous."

"Let's play a trick on them, shall we?"

"Oh, yes, let's!" The boy was joyful at this turn of events.

The tengu leaned down. "Call them all here. Tell them you have something to show them."

"But they'll see you!"

"No," the tengu promised. "They will only see you."

The boy did as was suggested and soon a large crowd had gathered at the base of the tree. The boy was pleased that the tengu's words were true. No one paid any notice to the hawk-nosed, winged creature.

"Now tell them to watch," the tengu prompted.

"Watch carefully, foolish people!" the boy trumpeted, standing on the branch, one hand on the tree trunk.

"Tell them that they will see something no one else has seen."

"You will see something no other person on this planet has *ever* seen!"

"Now fly."

"But . . ."

"Fly. Trust me. You can fly."

Hama was delighted. The anticipation was a tangible

thing in his mind and his body. He could feel the spark inside him. It practically lifted him off the branch. He was certain that he *could* fly. He would fly in the dream. He would soar!

"Watch!" he shouted and leaped from the branch.

The world sunk away from him. He could see for miles and miles. The ground stretched out in all directions. His stomach felt like it was turning over. His head was filled with the most expansive feeling he had ever experienced. He was flying!

For only a second.

The feeling left when the energy dissipated like an expanding gas ball. He started to sink. Hama tried to control his dream, willing himself up. But it didn't work. Horribly, he lost all control of the images. He fell, screaming and writhing.

He clawed at the air. His legs ran and kicked. The rushing air filled his mouth, choking him. His mind filled with the terrifying sensation of falling.

Then the tengu was laughing at *him*. "Trust me," it said. "You can fly."

He fell forever, then crashed into the ground.

His soul fell from the sky and slammed, clawing, back into his own body. His hand grabbed for his father's sword, which lay by the bed. He drove it up into his mother's body.

She was leaning over his prone form, her right elbow bent, her right arm raised. In her right hand was a tanto. She held it above her son's chest.

When the "ninja-to" blade pierced her, her intent

face relaxed. Her eyes closed as she dropped the dagger and clutched her stomach.

She leaned back, collapsing onto her haunches. Hama scrambled away, dragging the single futon covering with him. He crawled to the corner of the room, the bloodied blade in his hand, its bloody edge dragging along the floor—making a red line from the bed to him. It pointed like a tengu finger.

His mother grimaced, and then smiled. "I knew," she said. "I knew you would not fail us. We are..." She licked her lips. Hama could practically feel her internal organs hemorraging beneath her clutching, red-soaked fingers. The stain spread across her cool, light-blue kimono.

"We are very proud of you," she said. She fell forward, stiffly.

Hama never forgot the sickening sound of her face hitting the wood floor. It broke her nose. It cut her upper lip. It bruised her forehead.

She lay in the center of the severe room, across the bed. She looked like a puppet a careless child had dropped. Her ritualized makeup made her face a mask as well. A death mask. Her skin was white. Black lines encircled her eyes. Black lines were her eyebrows. Her lips were bright red. Her eyes were open.

The little boy, the young man, the yamabushi, and the tengu sat in the corner of the room, chanting quietly in the empty, dead house.

"The Hanshi is everything. The Hanshi is all. Never forget. The Hanshi is everything, the Hanshi is all..."

Outside, the wind laughed. "You can fly."

Outside, the kamikazes flew their planes into American ships.

Outside, the atomic bombs dropped on Nagasaki and Hiroshima.

In such a world, could anything not be believed?

"Trust me," said the tengu. "You can fly."

PART TWO
YUKI-ONNA

A woman, a dog, and a walnut-
tree,
The more you beat 'em, the better
they be.

Thomas Fuller

A woman always has her revenge ready.

Molière

4

Unspeakable torture. Literally unspeakable—they did not speak of it. It was a wall of feelings. It was a phrase. *Cha-no-yu*. Hot water for tea.

In the spring, with the earth awakened with the heavens' tears of rain, *cha-no-yu*.

In the summer, when the sun's rage tears the earth's skin, *cha-no-yu*.

In the autumn, when southern winds blow the rich orange, red, and yellow leaves, *cha-no-yu*.

And now, when the north winds frost the ground and the burnt hues of the flowers break the glass, *cha-no-yu*.

> Cha-no-yu,
> Like distant spring,
> created in beauty,
> for the pleasure it brings.

No, terrible, completely wrong. She dare not show that to her.

> All of nature's beauty,
> nothing in reserve,
> is the truth of being,
> the Lord which I serve.

The count was still wrong. Six, six, twelve, then thirteen . . . like the poem of Fujiwara no Teika:

> Where are the crimson leaves,
> Flowers of the season?
> Only a little hut on the long curving bay
> Stands in the serenity of an autumn evening.

That was what she wanted. That was what she demanded of her. And a pale plagiarism would not suffice. The girl had already tried that, months back.

> Here are the ground leaves,
> wonders of tradition,
> but a tiny key to the lock of oneself,
> opening the way to the sky and the warmth of the sun.

The woman had torn that into dozens of pieces, without anger, without disgust, without any visible emotion, and thrown it to the ground. The girl had to clean up every little piece from the petals of the garden flowers. Although the woman had seemed expressionless, the girl could feel the weight of the woman's disappointment along her shoulders, through her neck, and into her temples.

The feeling was there again. She could not hope to create a new poem that rivaled the beauty and simplicity of the late master. She had to be content with copying his words, once again, on the scroll paper, with the calligraphy brush. She had to put her own poetry writing aside to complete the kakemono in time.

So much to do, but she could not afford to rush. She had to do things quickly, but she could never hurry. The woman could instantly see when she had rushed things. The kakemono calligraphy scrolls had to be created and hung in the tea room alcove with as much care as the rest of the ceremony. Or else. Or else . . .

She emptied her body of all emotion, driving her anxiousness to her brain—where it belonged. The jolts of doubt and fear pressed against her brow, as her fingers gripped the ink-soaked brush, then gracefully moved it from paint to paper. The Japanese character-letters seemed to take shape with inspiring ease, but her eyes only saw imperfections.

Dread seemed to crawl from the blackness of the drying ink onto her hands like a fist-sized spider. She remained motionless so it would not bite and poison her. It crawled up her arms and under her chin. She waited for any further movement, her neck getting damp from the strain. But the next thing she felt was the stabs in her brain.

As always, they came on the right and left sides simultaneously. These stabs were echoed by one more at the crest of her right arm, like a sharp insect sting. She glanced at her dark-clad shoulder to see the bone-white ivory needle sticking there.

She bowed instantly, burying her face over her hands. Her mother turned away, the punishment for the girl's sloppy calligraphy work and lack of poetic inspiration already administered.

The woman was tall and stiffly beautiful, looking hardly older than her fifteen-year-old daughter. Only the face had hardened into a distant state—slowly hollowing over the years. With every passing season, her cheekbones seemed to get higher and her cheeks more sunken. Her eyes narrowed and her hair became flatter and darker.

The hands remained the same. The elegant, flowing, impossibly agile and nimble hands. They could do anything with a dexterity that was astonishing to watch. The girl remembered fighting back tears when she first saw her mother serving tea to her father in the cha-no-yu ceremony. The subtlety and the wonder was breathtaking.

But now the father was gone, and the fingers held nothing but the needles. They were gloriously carved with intricate patterns and symbols along their tapering hilts—a magnificent accomplishment by the artisan— but each ended in the incredibly sharp point. Points so amazingly thin, but still decorated by a wondrously small red dot at their bases.

The father . . . the girl only had her memories of the man. Tall, wide, muscular, his broad, rough face topped by that amazing hair. The hair that was red and copper and wheat, all at the same time. The gray and red hair that seemed to roll along his brow over his eyes. The deep red and white hair on his arms and curling across his chest.

She dimly remembered nightmares about him. Fortified by her mother's stories, the nightmares were narrated by her mother's voice. He was a sailor, she said. He had raped her, she said. He had forced her to marry him, and as a good Japanese wife, she could not refuse to serve him. Serve him tea or anything else he demanded. He was a monster, she said.

But all the girl could recall was the love she felt every time she saw him, every time he hugged her, every time he called her name... "Riso," he said. "Riso, Riso, my ideal." Riso meant ideal in Japanese.

But he was gone, so long she began to doubt he ever existed. Her mother said the man she remembered never existed. He was a dream to save her from the recollection of her "real" father. Soon the woman stopped talking about him at all and forbade her daughter to speak or even think of the man. And the woman said that the girl's name was "Risu," not Riso. Riso meant ideal. Risu meant "squirrel."

Her mother now took her place before the "kyujigushi," the small opening in the wall which guests crawled through for the tea ceremony. Risu was on her "daime tatami" mat where implements had to be. They both wore traditional kimonos, both severe and exactingly prepared, only the daughter's was plain, while the mother's was luxurious. The same was true of their wooden sandals.

"Prepare," said the woman. "The guests will come soon."

The words were like a death knell. It had been a long time since they had had guests. That meant this cha-no-yu was a test to see what the girl had learned. The mother rose from her kneeling position and calmly walked over to where the scroll hung, giving Risu room to crawl from the room. She had much to do before she could return to the daime tatami.

Their tiny teahouse was set out in a distant, wooded area on the island of Ichi—set in the Pacific ocean, to the east of the main island of Honshu, directly east of the coastal town of Shimoda. The small enclosure was six mats big; that is, the floor space was covered by six mats, each with a different purpose and position.

Outside the enclosure was a grander design, however. There was the garden, which encircled the teahouse, an area as important as the ceremony room itself. This little circle of bamboo, rice paper, and plants seemed to be in its own world—Risu's world—but in truth, just beyond it was the family house. The severe, small, nearly empty family house. That was where the girl slept. From the moment she awoke until her mother said so, she honed her skills in the teahouse and tea garden.

The ritual had been "pricked" into her with the ivory pins—so often Risu began to think that her mother's fingernails were blood-dotted ivory.

First she had to see to the stepping stones—those rocks that kept the guests' feet from touching the dirt. They had artistic meaning as well as a purpose, as did everything in the ceremony.

Risu had to find them herself years ago, collecting the most interesting rocks from the mountains and riverbeds. She had to carry them for the approval of her mother. She needed ten, four for "watari," practicality, and six for "kei," appearance. For every stone that did not gain her mother's approval, a pinprick.

Finally the ten were collected and placed. Again, if the placing did not suit her mother, a pinprick. And even worse, the stone had to be dug up again and repositioned. The various sizes and shapes had to be placed artistically, so their alignment and relationship to each other "meant" something. As always, Risu could not understand what "meant" implied. What was she supposed to do?

Finally, her mother accepted a pattern that was aesthetically pleasing, not from their positioning, she said, but because of the rocks' intrinsic shapes. The girl could not understand that, either. All she really knew was that the first phase was over. It allowed Risu to start designing the plantings. She had to find and transport cedars, pines, and oaks in such quantity and position them so that her mother was satisfied. Once those were hand-planted, she encircled each with shrubs and grass.

Even then, she didn't know what aesthetic effect was achieved until everything reached full flower. At first she was extremely happy, and proudly displayed the spring foliage to her mother. The garden was a sumptuous wash of gently blending colors and mingling aromas. Her mother forced her to tear up everything. As she stabbed the pin into her arms, the woman scolded her.

"Nothing must distract the guests from the cha-no-yu! Not smells or sights. The ceremony must be beautiful above all!"

Risu replanted the entire garden. The next spring

her mother found it too plain. It lacked innate beauty. It was torn up again. Risu soon dreaded each spring's flowering, even years after the garden was set to her mother's satisfaction.

Soon after the trees and shrubs were set, her mother presented her with a new challenge. Between the plants she had to design moss arrangements. Risu had to collect white sand and pine needles first, creating fragile works of art on the ground that the wind could destroy at any time. Each morning, Risu had to reshape the patterns her mother had approved. Next came the tending of the moss, which could not overgrow the stones or the other plants.

On the day of the guests, the fifteen-year-old went outside to trim the moss and reshape the pine needles over the combed sand. Then she went to the well and brought a pail of water for the "tsukubai," wash basin. It was more of a small pool that Risu filled, checking the positions of the "yuoke-ishi," flat stone, where a pail of hot water had to be placed, and the "mae-ishi," crouching stone, upon which the guests kneeled to clean their hands in the pool.

To the side of the tsukubai was the "ishi-doro," stone lantern, which Risu had carefully positioned so the candle, once lit, would only illuminate the flat stones around the basin. She lifted the lantern's paper door and cleaned inside—preparing for the oil lamp to go inside what looked like a miniature stone pagoda.

From there, she went directly to the "chiri-ana," debris pit, which was decorated with flower petals. From inside her waistband, Risu took the special green bamboo chopsticks with which she cleaned the garden of fallen leaves. Each leaf was individually picked up by the chopsticks and dropped into the small, round pit. Risu then placed some twigs atop the leaves and left the chopsticks by the pit—as tradition dictated.

Tradition also dictated the watering of the garden; a process called "mizu s'toraiki"—water striking. It too was a delicate affair, where not a single drop could be displaced. Or else another pinprick and a repeat performance of the entire procedure.

Finally Risu felt secure enough to go back inside. There she had to tend to her "mei"—the personal utensils of the tea ceremony. She had made them all herself in years past—she had to. Her mother had left her no choice. Now she carefully checked their positioning and inventory. There was the "mizuashi," ceramic water jar, the "cha-ire," ceramic powdered-tea container, the "chashaku," tea ladle, the "chasen," tea whisk, the "kama," kettle, and the "hibashi," metal chopsticks for the charcoal.

The charcoal! She had to tend that next, taking the strange, log-shaped pieces of ornate, specially created charcoal and sawing off different shapes without making the edges uneven—so the pieces were smooth. That done, she was almost ready. All that was left now was to see to the flowers and incense.

It was January, so the mood and sky were dark. She decided that the flowers had to reflect the mood of the season. In the garden, set between her mother's house and the tea room, she selected winter peonies, camellias, and plum blossoms. She carefully arranged them in

the vase hanging on the inside wall of the daime tatami.
Next she had to choose the four different kinds of
incense her guests would sample and the burners in
which each would be contained.

She only stopped her preparations when she felt the
familiar pain between her shoulder blades.

"The guests are arriving," her mother said, removing
the pin tip from the girl's back.

Risu hastily retreated to light the welcoming candle.
She took it outside to meet the three men who were
coming up the path. Although he was not in front, the
small man with the thin, long, graying hair coming from
his upper lip, chin, and head, was obviously the leader
of the entourage. The other two were impressive, somber men, but they deferred to the gray man in speech
and manner. For his part, the little gray man spoke
casually and smiled.

When Risu had reached them within the garden, it
was he who wound up facing her, looking at her with a
mirthless smile of appraisal. She directed the three
men to the arbor, a small, roofed, three-sided alcove
where they were to wait until the woman rang the
gong—summoning them inside for the tea ceremony.
Without a word, Risu left them and went inside, careful
not to hurry.

Her heart was in her throat and she could feel her
breath coming faster. She knew just by looking at these
men that this cha-no-yu was important. And she could
tell, just by looking at her mother, that any fault with
the performance would be blamed on the performer . . .
not the director.

Looking away from her scurrying daughter, the woman hit the invitational gong with a padded mallet.

Risu served the guests sweet cakes on the ceremonial tray, being careful to bow very low on her knees before the men. They had entered silently, with reverence, and now they ate silently. Risu retreated to the preparation room, a screened-off area where the hostess must sit until the minor meal was finished.

Already the girl was panic-stricken. She had made the kashi cakes very carefully, following the ancient recipe. They were sweet dough filled with dark-purple, sweet bean paste. She had been very proud of them. They rose beautifully and were exactly the dark and light brown colors they were supposed to be.

She had used their best plates and positioned the cakes on each as finely as she could. The men were supposed to comment on the beauty and delicacy of all before them: the garden, the room, the hanging scroll she had labored on, the flowers she had arranged so carefully, and the food. They were supposed to actively appreciate all the trouble she had gone through. But all she heard was mastication.

When the sounds of their eating diminished, she steeled herself for the main show. She moved humbly into the room. They were where she had left them, sitting calmly along the guest tatami mat. She went to her place by the small, square fire pit built into the floor. All her utensils were set out in the proper manner. With an internal sigh, she started "temae"—the art of making and serving tea.

She threw herself into the act. She concentrated on

the lyrical beauty of all things. She paraded her memory of the process across a mental backdrop of cool, crystal streams running through gloriously snow-capped mountains. She molded the ash with an ash spoon in the small portable brazier. The tea ladle swept into her hands like a trained pet. She set it down in its preassigned place with exacting precision.

She wiped the tea scoop with the "fukusa," silk cloth, then warmed the tea bowl with hot water. After she had poured that out, she wiped the bowl dry with a white linen cloth. Only then could she spoon the powdered green tea out of the lacquered tea caddy and into the tea bowl. Each movement of her body had to be considered the finest choreographed dance. Her movements had to "speak" for her artistic soul.

The ladle had to be handled precisely, each finger coming into play and hitting exact positions. With it she poured boiling water atop the fire pit into the tea bowl. Then the water had to be poured into the kettle. Finally the water was added to the tea. Risu tried not to think of the process, just let instinct and logic take over. She could feel the men's eyes on her. She could feel her mother sticking the ivory pins into her temples from inside her brain.

Then she saw her father. The man with the laughing green eyes and fiery hair. He was smiling at her from far away. He stood, waiting for her to make him proud. Risu swirled the ladle onto the rim of the kettle as she was supposed to.

Then came the ritual of laying charcoal. She lifted the kettle smoothly. She sprinkled the wet ash over the ash already inside the pit. Then, from a basket, she took the largest piece of charcoal she had carved and placed it in the pit by hand. She decorated the remainder of the pit bottom with the smaller charcoal pieces, using the metal chopsticks.

Her mind was singing now. She felt satisfied with her performance. It was flowing and each step came into her mind effortlessly. The charcoal finished, she next wiped the tea caddy, handling the silk wiping cloth according to the set method her mother had painstakingly taught her.

Then, with a barely perceptible flourish, she poured the powdered tea into the tea bowl. Then the boiling water was ladled in. Then the mixture was whisked with the chasen. Then she waited, letting the serenity of nature fill her body. She almost meditated, waiting for the proper aroma of steeped tea to reach her nostrils. When it was finally ready, she elegantly offered the bowl to the little gray man.

After he had carefully taken the bowl from her, she repositioned the instruments carefully, so each was in full view of the guests. Then she leaned back on her bended knees, letting an interior sigh rattle through her body and ricochet through her mind. It was finished. All she had to do now was sit there, allowing the guests to enjoy the refreshment.

Her reverie was broken by the gray man's word. "Tagashi," he said.

She dare not look at him. Instead she sensed the approach of her mother, who entered and sat on her knees before the man.

"Hanshi," she said.

He reached out and gently motioned for the woman to move aside so he could have a clear view of the child. "Please," he started, speaking directly to Risu. "Tell me about the ritual."

If his words had been spat with angry intensity, they would have had the same effect. The girl had no choice but to speak. "Temae was created by the warlord's attendant," she started, her voice mechanical as she recited her lessons, "who had to protect the family's most valued possessions and serve tea in a graceful manner. The originator of temae was Shuko, who taught the spiritual meaning of the ceremony to his students. He concentrated his mind on the gestures."

"The intent?" the Hanshi inquired. Risu said nothing, her mind frozen. Intent? Intent? "The result?" the Hanshi suggested.

"Unaffectation," she said. "Inconspicuousness." Risu felt wounded. The Hanshi had to ask her a *second* question. Her silence had been the deepest pinprick of all. The needles lanced through her skull into her brain. Her temples pounded like drums.

"Continue," the Hanshi said. "The three elements?"

"Arrangement, Purification, Serenity."

"Arrangement?"

"Carrying and positioning the utensils properly."

"Purification?"

"Cleaning the tea bowl, cleaning the tea caddy, cleaning the tea scoop. Warming the bowl. Wiping it."

"Serenity?"

"Time," Risu remembered. "Time between kaiseki and temae. Between serving and cleaning."

The Hanshi nodded, then purposely dropped his bowl to the tatami. The thin green tea still in the cup splashed out.

He might as well have ripped Risu open.

" 'Squirrel' is not a name," he said to the woman. "It denotes something. Her name is nothing. 'Rei-a.' 'All of nothing.' " He looked directly at the despairing girl. "You are Rhea."

The Hanshi moved his body over and unceremoniously crawled out of the room through the kyujigushi. His two associates followed him without a word, without an expression. The woman followed them. Risu heard them leaving the teahouse. She stared at the vase of flowers, at the poetry scroll. She stared at the bowl laying on its side on the tatami, liquid drooling from it as if it had been stabbed.

Risu fainted.

All the world was snow. Rhea stood in it, up to her calves. Her legs were wrapped with white cloth, her feet with black cloth. Over her torso was a sleeveless dark-blue padded jacket. Her arms and hands were wrapped the same way her legs were. She saw herself, her expression tight, her long black hair twisting in the howling wind.

She stood on a crest. Behind her was another crest. Before her were many more. Lying at her feet was a dead man facedown. Dotting the hills beyond her were more men, their shirts dark, their pants dark, their hair dark. They looked like dozens of corpses of the same man.

She looked down at the man before her. The wind began to move the snow across his back. The wind was burying him. The wind buried them one by one until none were left. Then Rhea saw another man in the distance. He was not dead, not lying on his face in the snow. He was walking upright, looking up at the most beautiful woman Rhea had ever seen.

She was extraordinary. At first Rhea saw her as angelic. But though she was majestic, there was something about her that precluded the heavenly image. It was the way she carried herself, the way she moved through the snow.

Her flawless form was wrapped in white and rose silk that flowed in the air behind her. The wind also blew her silken hair that danced across her gentle features. She did not so much walk as flow. And every move she made was effortless elegance.

The man walked beside her, fighting the elements to stare reverently at her. Rhea called to them, but they did not seem to hear. She called again, louder. The pair simply moved on, perpendicular to her. She shouted once more, as loud as she could.

Only the woman seemed to notice. She looked directly at Rhea, irritably. Her expression told the girl to be quiet. Something in her face made Rhea want to contact the man all the more. She screamed at the top of her lungs again and again.

The woman stared at Rhea until the man noticed her gaze. He seemed about to turn toward Rhea when the woman cooed at the man, holding his head in both her hands. She cupped his face, slowly sitting in the storm as if it were a spring picnic. The man lay beside her, his head in her lap. She stroked him until his eyes closed.

Rhea watched and screamed as the man slowly died, a smile on his face. Rhea only quieted for the moment of the man's death. Her voice died in a hoarse rattle as the woman set the man's head down in the snow. She leaned across his middle and breathed over his face. When she inhaled, his soul went into her body.

She rose to her full height across from Rhea, who shrank back. The woman melted.

When Rhea turned, the woman stood before her.

She was demure, the most exquisite creature Rhea had ever seen. She held the end of her resplendent mane in her hands, caressing it gently. An innocent smile played on her lips. The wind howled around them, the snow rippling like water.

"I will let you live," the woman said. Rhea said nothing. "You have no questions?" Rhea had been painfully taught to accept everything and question nothing. So the woman spoke for them both.

"Why do I let you live? Because I like to laugh. You are a funny little girl. You live in a world that is not reality and not dreams."

"Who are you?" Rhea finally asked.

"Who do you think, silly girl?" the woman said, spreading her arms, her silk sleeves like wings. "The Snow Woman."

"Yuki-onna," Rhea breathed. "You have come for me."

"I have come *to* you, foolish girl. I only come *for* young men dying in the mountain snow. I bring sleep and death only to them."

"Take me too," Rhea begged.

"No, foolish girl."

"Please!"

"You are a coward. You could come to me, but will not."

"I can not!"

"Will not," the Snow Woman repeated petulantly. "You live in fear though you remember love. You can choose between love and fear, but will not."

"I remember love. I have only fear."

"All of nothing, little one. Little one, all of nothing. I will not come to you again." The Snow Woman began to melt.

"Don't leave me!"

"You will walk in my footsteps," said the Yuki-onna's voice. "You will not have to look. Wherever you step will be my step."

The Snow Woman was gone. Rhea stood on the hilltop, the tiny shurikens of sleet cutting into her like pinpricks.

Rhea awoke to the needles. Her mother jabbed them in again and again as she lay on the floor of the teahouse.

"Horrid girl!" the woman spat. "The Hanshi had never been so insulted! Our family has never been so shamed!"

"Mother!" Rhea cried in anguish, the pins dotting

her arms, her hands, her shoulders, her stomach, her thighs, her breasts, her face. "I did my best!"

"Your best!" the mother cried. Pinprick. "All the utensils were made from the same spicebush tree!" Pinprick. "The stone lantern was lit in winter!" Pinprick.

"The flowers were the same hue!" Pinprick. The colors should have melded.

"The implements had no bearing on the season!" Pin. They "meant" nothing.

"The bowls were all ceramic!" Pin. They should have been different materials.

"The caddy and water jar were both tall!" Pin. One should have been flat.

"The kettle and charcoal pot were both round!" Pin. One should have been square.

The great tea master of the 1500's, Sen no Rikyu, was once asked how the host of cha-no-yu should act. He replied: "It is correct for the host to do his best to please his guest, but incorrect to *try* to do so."

When Rhea awoke the following day, her body was a mass of tiny puncture wounds. Every movement caused pain. She had been raised strictly, however. She forced herself to do the same chores she had been doing for ten years. She wasn't even aware it was the morning of her sixteenth birthday.

But she became aware of the house's emptiness. Her mother was gone. She searched the entire grounds but there was no sign of her. Even though every movement brought renewed pain, Rhea was numbed by the realization of her persecutor's disappearance. All she remembered of her life was her mother and her mother's teachings. Now she was certain that her failure the previous night was going to destroy her.

Her mother had deserted her. And without the skills of cha-no-yu, Rhea was destined to become a geisha in a miserable hotel or brothel. Or worse, a prostitute in a garish bar catering to American soldiers on leave from Vietnam. Even on the minuscule island of Ichi, time could not be slowed. It was 1965 and Rhea could see no future. Her mother had brainwashed her well. Her numbed mind offered no hope.

She sat in the tea garden miserably, pondering her fate. After several hours, she vacuously decided. As far as she was concerned, she had only one real choice. She would search out the Hanshi and ask for another chance. By afternoon she had tended her wounds, changed into a clean kimono, and gathered her belongings. They consisted of a pair of metal chopsticks, a jade comb, a hairpin, and a folding, collapsible fan.

On the afternoon of her sixteenth birthday, Rhea Tagashi set out to find the Hanshi.

5

He waited for her over the hills and across the ocean. He waited for her in Shimoda, between the Sagami Sea and Suruga Bay, on the Ito Peninsula. He waited for her as the ninja dogged her trail, moving behind, beside, and above her—following and leading—without her ever noticing.

Instead she noticed the glorious beauty of her homeland. The cold winds assailed her and the snow infiltrated her clothes to wet her skin, but that couldn't defeat her appreciation of the winter country.

It was so peaceful, so quiet, so . . . light. Winter was almost weightless, even when the snow hung heavily on the tree branches, pushing them toward the ground. The spring was crisp, before the camphor and holly trees could bloom. The summer was at first bright, and then drenched with the "baiu"—the "plum rain" that fell in torrents as the plum trees gave fruit. The autumn was clear—better to see the dense green of the pines and the rainbow earth-oceans of newly dead leaves.

But now snow lay on everything in a rolling blanket of white. The brown of the earth and tree bark created natural highlights, living artwork for Rhea. She let the sights fill her head, driving out all other thought. Driving out almost everything, including the sensory hints that would have revealed the ninja who cavorted all around her.

They escorted her without her knowledge, paving her way with misery. She walked until she reached the island's port. She decided to rest there and partake of a cup of tea before she sought out the ferry for a ride across. She carried her belongings to a small building that nestled on the corner facing the wharf. The kimonoed hostess—a plain, flat-faced girl with crooked teeth but kind eyes, cheerily let her in.

Neither saw the man in back with the innkeeper. He had slipped through the rear door and was feeding the innkeeper's hand with oblong silver disks. When the hostess, the innkeeper's niece, called that they had a customer, the two men hastily concluded their business, the ninja hunching down as he slipped out the back and the innkeeper shoving the coins into his sleeve and marching out from behind the counter.

"Who is this?" he cried, waving off the hostess at the same time.

"A customer!" the hapless girl screeched, moving quickly away like a dog who had been beaten too often.

"I only want a cup of tea," Rhea began. The innkeeper turned on her.

" 'I only want a cup of tea,' " he mimicked, fists on his hips, his head waving, leaning over. "That's what all of them want! Do you have any money to pay for this tea?"

The niece gasped. This was a terrible breach of etiquette.

"Quiet, you!" he exclaimed, turning to his hostess. "No good girl is out walking alone this time of year. I know her type. If I serve you, they'll all start coming in here!" He turned back to Rhea. "Well?"

Rhea couldn't return his gaze. Instead she started to go through her things for something of value. "I . . ." she began.

"I thought so!" the innkeeper concluded. "Out!"

She found herself back in the cold, facing the water with nothing to warm her and little in the way of prospects. She went to boatman after boatman until she found an old man who would take her jade comb for a ride across to Shimoda.

The ride was uneventful. And once she stepped onto mainland soil, she was back at square one. It was still cold, she was still hungry, and she had no money.

Each shopkeeper she questioned told her the same thing. No, they had never seen anyone that fit her description of the old, small, gray-haired man. But a pretty girl who needed money could always visit the Ficus Inn for lodgings and a job. As Rhea wandered away, almost all of them felt the silver in their pockets, wondering who would play such an elaborate joke on such a sweet-looking young girl?

The Ficus Inn was down a narrow alley, away from the street leading up from the docks. The enclosed space squeezed the wind into a battering ram of air that tore at her as she hurried along. The same rice-papered walls lined the streets, differentiated by the paper lanterns hanging from the awning of each two-story building. She saw the character-letter marking the Ficus, and hurried inside.

She slid the door closed behind her and turned. She found herself standing on an upraised platform. Spread before her was a smoke-filled room filled with staring men. They sat on the floor around tables and on benches built into the walls. Small white jugs of sake seemed to be in every hand and on every table. But every eye was on her.

The roar of conversation dimmed for a minute, then burst forth with renewed vigor. They turned to each other and cheered her. A squat but burly man came forward and put his arm around her shoulder.

"Come, come, my dear!" he said. "You must be freezing! Come closer to the fire!"

He directed her to a brazier in the middle of the room, over which hung a kettle. From it came the delicious aroma of soybean soup. Until that moment, Rhea didn't realize how hungry she was.

"Like some?" the man said. His hair was black and thin, his eyes were small, too close together, and his teeth were also black—not to mention crooked.

"Yes, please," Rhea heard herself say. She was too

tired and too hungry to argue. She would take his hospitality and cross what bridges he erected when she came to them.

After the soup, he offered and she ate a bowl of noodles. The time between the meal and him leading her upstairs seemed negligible. She followed him along a dark hallway to a dusty, insect-infested room with ripped rice-paper walls.

"Nice, eh?" he commented, lighting a candle which sat in a tin holder on a stool by the door. He showed her the two shelves that served as a closet, and the lumpy mattress on the floor that served as a bed. "You can stay here as long as you like," he said, "provided."

Rhea was still tired, but the food had taken the edge off her head. "Provided?" she inquired, on the far side of the room.

The man closed the door and spread his arms wide. "Provided you help out," he said with a smile. "We need a new girl."

Rhea visibly relaxed. "Oh, yes," she agreed. "I will be glad to help out. I can . . . I can do cha-no-yu."

"Excellent!" the man said, getting closer. "Yes, by all means." He was very near her now. She could smell him. She was beginning to feel sick.

"Please," she said. He was standing before her, blocking the light. She couldn't see his face.

"Oh," he suddenly said. "I'm sorry." He backed away, his expression showing concern. "You must be exhausted. I understand. You should rest." He motioned toward the mattress. "Please," he invited.

"Thank you," Rhea said, waiting. He smiled warmly, then left the room.

It was warm there, baked by the sweaty activity downstairs. Rhea was almost becoming faint again. She decided not to try undoing the kimono tonight. She quickly lay on the mattress, its bumps feeling like massaging hands in her state. She rolled onto her side, put her arms beneath her head, and closed her eyes.

The Yuki-onna stood on the mountain top, the wind blowing her rose gown and jet-black hair.

Again, Rhea was captivated by her beauty and serenity.

But almost at the same moment, disquiet interrupted her thoughts. She peered across the great distance.

It was not serenity that marked the Snow Woman's face. The expression was deep-set, initially unfathomable. As she let her cascading hair drift through her fingers, her eyes moved slowly until she was looking directly back at the little girl.

Inside those eyes, lighting them from behind, was hate. A pure, undiluted hatred.

Rhea's own eyes seemed to retreat. She could not bear to see such powerful emotion, but she could not turn away. Instead her view became distant. The Snow Woman began to get smaller. She shrank until Rhea could see her shoulders, then her torso, then her entire body framed in the distance.

And still, the view changed. Rhea saw the Yuki-onna's feet planted wide on the mountaintop. A white-capped mountaintop.

But it was not the white of snow. It was the white of . . . flesh.

Rhea moaned. The Snow Woman was standing on a mountaintop. A mountain of corpses. A mountain of dead men.

Rhea closed her eyes and screamed in anguish.

A rough hand slapped down over her lips.

Rhea tried to knock the clamping fingers away, but her arms seemed embedded in tar. They moved with an initial jerk and then slowed. She kicked, but her knees would bend only slightly. She felt pressure. . . . She felt . . . pain.

Her eyes snapped open. Her vision was completely filled with the sweaty, leering face of the man who had showed her the room.

Her eyes rolled in their sockets. The men were all around her, filling the room. They held onto her ankles and arms as the man tore at her kimono. She screamed for help, hearing the words disappear in a man's meaty hand like so many drops of spittle.

She writhed on the floor, kicking and screeching.

The man pulling layer after layer of her kimono aside looked over at the man who squeezed the girl's mouth. "You like that, eh?" he grunted.

The man nodded, smiling, liking the feeling of her lips moving beneath his palm. "Hurry up," he said.

"They have to wait," the man said between deep breaths. "All good things take time. Hold her still, will you!" The others watched as he pulled the underlayers aside—each getting thinner as he neared her kicking legs.

All the men gasped in appreciation when they reached

them—young, smooth, shapely. The pinpricks were hardly noticeable. The man looked back at the others with a face that said "See? What did I tell you? Buried treasure!" Japanese women were so completely covered that the sight of skin could drive weaker men almost mad with lust.

Rhea was in a room crowded with some of the weakest. The man scrambled back on his knees, clawing at his own belt. "Hold her," he grunted. "Hold her still."

"Iie!" Rhea cried against the hand, her head rising, her neck muscles straining. Sweat poured from her brow, making the man's gagging grip slippery. "Iie, iie!"

No, no.

Hands were on her wrists, around her upper arms. Her elbows were bent. She was on her back. Hands started tearing at her upper kimono as the man pushed his pants down. He angrily jerked forward, slapping their hands away.

"You'll get your chance later!" he scolded. "My turn first!" He triumphantly grabbed at her final undergarment and tore it from her hips.

The men cheered and laughed with pleasure and anticipation. Between her legs was a smooth, straight, inch-wide band of hair surrounded by smooth pink skin. The men stamped their feet and hooted.

Rhea shook her head over and over as the man slowly laid himself across her body. The man was completely atop her now. He slapped at the hand over her mouth.

"Come on, I want to taste her."

"She might bite," the gagging man said, disappointed.

"She won't bite."

"Someone might hear her!"

"So what?"

The man lay one arm across Rhea's throat and used the other to grind at her chest through her kimono top.

"Please," she gasped. "Please. I am . . . I am a virgin."

The men couldn't believe their good fortune. Her choked announcement was greeted by renewed celebration. The man on top of her merely smiled.

"Not for long," he said. He reached down to guide his already stiff member to her vagina.

"It's dry," he said. Rhea had shut her eyes, turning her head away. "Your loss," he shrugged.

He forced his penis inside her, pushing and thrusting. He twisted at her kimono top. "Relax," he said, jerking, tearing at her parched insides. "Relax. You might like it."

His words reached the window and went no farther. But it was far enough for the three men lying on the sloped ceiling to hear. They would occasionally lower themselves until they could see the rapists' progress. But they did nothing.

The words echoed in Rhea's ears. She screwed her eyes shut even tighter and gritted her teeth. The pain should not have been as bad as the anguish, but that just wasn't true. It was a frightening pain, made all the worse from never having felt it before. It was inside her! It wasn't a needle puncturing her skin. It was inside! Inside!

"Come on," the man said. "Come on, come on, relax. Just relax." But she was a motionless piece of meat below him, tears streaming from her closed eyes. Her only movement was an occasional spasm of terror.

"Katsu," the man instructed, looking over at a man by the door. He motioned and the doorman understood. He brought the candle over as the others made way and chattered excitedly. The doorman slowly tipped it over Rhea's right leg. The liquid wax dripped down onto her exposed flesh.

The new pain shocked her—like a whip hitting a reluctant colt. She fought against the hands madly, almost breaking free of their grip. But they managed to hold on while other hands applauded her attempt and her torture.

It was too late to retreat inside her mind now. She was hysterical. She fought with all her strength, but even the weakest man in the room was stronger than her. He kept raping her and another dropped hot wax on her as she fought—making little wax coins over her quivering skin.

When she could think again, the man was still on top of her, thrusting. To her amazement, the pain was almost gone. She was shocked to find that her vagina was wet. She could hardly feel the man's member anymore.

The other men seemed to have sensed it. They had stopped their candle torture to cheer the man on to climax. She found him staring at her.

"You see?" he grunted, smiling. "I told you."

She remembered what he had said. She remembered very well. She leaned her head back, biting her lower lip. Then she began to make noise. And not screams for help, either.

"She likes it!" the man on top of her cried. "You see! She likes it!"

Rhea began to gasp, and make little cries. She started to move her hips with him. Just a little at first.

The others hooted at the ceiling and howled to the night. This was going to be fun!

Rhea leaned her head up and kissed the man. She kissed his cheeks, his chin, and his lips. She had to rest her head every few seconds to quell the "pleasure." Then she licked at his neck and face.

"She's an animal!" he cried with pleasure. "She *loves* it!"

She started to call out "suggestions." She gasped for him to do different things.

"My breasts," she gasped. "Please, please . . ."

"What?" the man teased. "What do you want me to do with your breasts?"

"Please," she begged. "Feel my . . . rub my breasts."

The man looked to the others with a smile that threatened to rip his head off at the ears. He opened her kimono like a curtain. He ripped at her undershirt until her round, full chest was revealed.

The unexplainable lust for tits gripped the men in a sex frenzy. They could barely contain themselves and the room could barely contain them. If Rhea had screamed at the top of her lungs just then, their delirium would have swallowed it like a whale eating a guppy.

The man squeezed them.

"No," Rhea suddenly panted. "Not like that."

"What?" the man wheezed, taken aback. "How?" He tried squeezing the nipple, sucking at it.

"No," Rhea pleaded. "Not like that."

"How? How?" he demanded feverishly. "Tell me!"

"Like this, like this," she said, trying to move her hand. The man slapped the restraining arms away. Rhea instantly grabbed his hand and laid it on her left breast. She slowly, gently moved it in a circular pattern. "Like that," she cooed with pleasure. "Just like that."

"Aah," said all the men, nodding in approval. The man on top of the girl looked at the others with pride. Rhea feigned satisfaction, slipping her hand off his.

Her head went back and then forward, as if she were trying to force him even deeper inside her.

He turned back to smile beneficently at his conquest.

Rhea clamped her teeth onto his lower lip.

She pulled the metal chopsticks from her waistband.

She rammed the sharpened tips deep into his left eye.

The man reared back, screaming.

He slammed into the men holding her legs.

She jammed the needles into the man holding her left arm.

He fell back. The man who had gagged her tried to grab her.

She slipped between his fingers and spun as she got to her feet. She kicked him in the face.

All the men fell back.

As the kicked man hit the floor, blood pouring from his mashed nose, Rhea dove forward, burying the sharpened chopstick points into the neck of the man holding the candle.

He stumbled back, gurgling, the needles still in his neck, as Rhea pressed the candle flame to the rice paper wall.

One man shouted and tried to stop her. Rhea pulled the long hairpin from her mane and cut him across the face.

The needle scraped across his eyelids and the bridge of his nose. He fell squirming, his hands on his face.

The wall caught fire.

Rhea dropped the candle and faced the men.

She stood, her kimono ripped off her chest and legs, her long hair hanging, a long pin clenched tightly in her right hand, the wall behind her engulfed in flames.

They fell over each other trying to get out of the burning room.

The man who had raped her was not dead. He held his hand to his ruined eye, blood streaming between his fingers. He stood before the hall window, just outside the open door to her room.

"Do something!" he yelled at the night.

A single arm appeared. The black-covered fingers grabbed him by the hair. With a single yank, the man was propelled out the window. He fell to the alley floor head first, crushing his skull. To the others it looked as if the man had jumped out the window. To the authorities who would appear some minutes later, he was just another corpse.

Rhea made it to the hall, backing the men off with the needle. They fell down the stairs, scrambling for the door. Rhea made it to the stair's first landing when the first man reached the exit.

He pulled it open, then flew backward.

His arms and legs were wide as he sailed through the air. He crashed to the wooden floor and slid to the opposite wall. His head went through the rice paper and he lay still.

A little, gray-haired man stood in the doorway, one arm out, his hand flat.

"Hanshi!" Rhea breathed.

The men charged him.

The Hanshi swept his two arms wide, knocking the first pair of men aside. He stood and delivered a vicious side kick to the jaw of the third, who flew back into two more—knocking all three down.

He kicked again, back. He kicked again front, he kicked again, side—all without putting his foot down once. Three men were catapulted in the three directions, slamming into the wall, a table, and the floor.

Rhea vaulted the steps' banister, landing near the soup kettle. She gripped its handle and swung it at the backs of the rest of the men. The Hanshi hid his face behind his kimono's wide sleeve as the hot liquid splashed against the men. They screamed and writhed.

The Hanshi marched through them, knocking them aside, until he was next to the girl.

"I shall do it, my child," he promised.

He took the empty kettle from her and used it as a martial arts weapon. It spun, twirled, and jumped in his hand, slamming each man in the face, on the head, against the throat. They fell like chopped trees until only Rhea and the Hanshi stood in the burning tavern.

"Hanshi," Rhea said in worship, falling to her knees, her arms around his legs.

"No, my child," he said soothingly, helping her up. She looked into his kind, concerned eyes.

"It took so long to find you," he said.

6

Some say the world will end in fire, while others think the world will end in ice. For Rhea Tagashi, the world *started* in ice.

All the loneliness of her childhood and the horror of her rite of passage was swallowed by the ice. It was a natural extension for her. From the snows of Ichi and Shimoda to the ice of Chiba.

It was only about a hundred miles from the coastal town where she had been raped to the town outside Tokyo where the Hanshi ran the ninja school. Just a short jaunt up the coast on the underbelly of Japan.

The ninja *school*. It was a laughable name for the place. It made it sound like a building that had a cafeteria, a gym, a drama club, and a prom. To call it anything would be ultimately laughable. What was it, an experience—the way a hot tub was an experience? It is to laugh.

It was not a building. It was more a compound. It was practically its own village. It seemed to be as large as the island of Ishi. It had tall stone walls surrounding it and lyrical pagodas sprinkled throughout. It had tiny dwellings made from the most beautiful of materials. It was simple, it was elegant.

The Hanshi himself didn't call it a "ryu." Nor did he call it "ninjutsu"—the art of stealth. He wasn't teaching an art class. He wasn't teaching. He ordered, he demanded. And he didn't call it anything.

Rhea thought of it as "sh'kata"—the way. The way out of her pain, the way out of her despair. It saved her from the fate worse than death and gave her something nothing else could—ice.

She vaguely remembered sitting in the small, airy, bright room, trying to overcome her shame and regret. She had failed the Hanshi at the tea ceremony. She had killed men at the tavern. She had been foully spoiled.

The world went on but Rhea sank into a mental snakepit of paralyzing guilt. Until the ice came.

It was winter. The world outside struggled. Japan itself ranted against the Vietnam conflict. It escaped the shackles of its World War Two shame and started regaining economic pride. But inside the Chiba compound Rhea sat.

The Hanshi came to her. He told her to get up. He brought her from her small dwelling out to the tiny garden. There, held up on two small tables, was a six-by-three-foot block of ice. It lay between the tiny, leafless trees—in the center of a triangle made by three stone shrines.

"You cannot continue your existence," the Hanshi judged. "You must start again." He pointed to the ice. "Make a person."

The Hanshi walked past her, but just before he left the yard, he reached into his sleeve and jammed a small but incredibly sharp two-sided, wood-handled knife into the ice.

Rhea stared blankly at the frozen monolith for many minutes—until she too looked frozen. But then she moved forward. She took the knife in her hand. She pulled it from the ice with an effort. She looked at the blade—glinting in the cold morning sun—as if to use it on herself. But then she stabbed the ice.

Once, then again, then again and again and again. She stabbed it repeatedly, using all her strength. She started gasping as she struck, then shrieking, finally grunting. She stopped when she sank to her knees in the snow.

She looked up. The sunlight refracted through the ice. She had hardly marred it. The top was pockmarked, but that was all. She touched the slick undersurface. Somewhere inside she saw her own reflection. Somewhere inside she saw gems. Somewhere inside she saw a future.

She did not have to tend the garden, she did not have to make tea. She did not have to fuck men. She didn't even have to carve a person from the ice block. But . . . but . . .

Rhea wrapped her cold fingers around the knife hilt.

She stood and stared at the ice block. Then she started to chip away at it.

Every morning it would be there. If it had snowed the night before, she would sweep the powder off with her sleeve and continue her work. She whittled the first block down to an unrecognizable mass. The second block was carved away to nothing. The third block broke in the middle and shattered on the hard ground.

But every day she would rise and one would be there. Every day she would go into the garden and toil on the ice block. All her concentration, everything she knew and had learned went into her sculpture. She chipped, she chopped, she cut away at the frozen water until it started to take shape.

First a vague mass that could be recognized as a body. Then the legs. Then the arms. Then the feet. Then the hands. Then, the hands some more. The fingers. The fingernails. Back to the toes. The chest. The neck. The head. Finally the face. The hair, the mouth, the nose, and the eyes. She labored on the eyes until they stared up at her, clear and glassy.

No sex organs. It was a person, not a man or a woman. She finished her first complete person, but destroyed it before the Hanshi could see. The next morning there was another block of ice. She worked on her second person for just a few weeks before destroying that. She didn't wait for the next morning to start the next. She asked for another block immediately.

For Rhea, the winter was every season. All she knew was the cold, although she no longer felt it. She didn't feel the years passing. She didn't notice her strength growing, she didn't realize her understanding was deepening. She didn't realize her balance was becoming exact, her eye for detail extraordinary.

She finished her first satisfactory person. She did not have to call the Hanshi. He was there. She turned and there he was. From beside him came the two men who had accompanied him at the tea ceremony. Without a word, they took the sculpture and lifted it to a vertical position. It actually stood before Rhea. Her creation stood before its maker.

The Hanshi looked at it. He walked toward it. As he was directly in front of it, he suddenly pulled a spike—a "tonki"—from his sleeve and drove it into the ice's eye, temple, ear, nostril, mouth, and neck. Each jab made a hole in the sculpture. Then he left the garden, without a word to the girl. His associates followed him.

There was no despair this time. She knew she had not failed. She walked into her dwelling, at first confused. But then she saw her sharpened metal chopsticks lying on her bed mat. She understood.

Each day she would train on the iceman. She would practice jabbing the needles into the holes so precisely that they did not touch the sides. She practiced doing it faster and faster, until her movements were a blur. On that day, the Hanshi returned to her.

There was no magic in this. He walked into the garden and surveyed the work as he had secretly every night since she started. In the nights, he could see the marks her chopsticks made. He merely waited until there were no more marks outside the holes. He appeared to her the next day.

He took a single look at the iceman. Then he shattered it with one blow. Rhea watched it collapse in nine ragged pieces with satisfaction. She smiled as it was destroyed. She looked from the pile of unrecognizable ice to the Hanshi's placid face.

"Come," he said. "Dine with me."

They ate together from that day on. As they ate across a small wooden table from each other, both seated on the bamboo mat on the floor, amid a wide, low room, exquisitely decorated with beautiful art scrolls, he played with a fan. He would flip it open and use it to cool himself in the summer.

His movements would be intricate but so precise they looked casual. Hot summer days he would swirl the fan, making lovely patterns before Rhea's eyes. Her fan would be lying beside her on the mat. She too would cool herself. She would dine with him, then cool herself the remainder of the day, creating physical poetry in the air with the fan.

The summers were long and hot, the winters long and cold. They blended together until the ice and the fan were one. She made the persons and he made the new targets until she had mastered a hundred and six points on the body.

And with each new block of ice, she would begin with a ritual where she jumped to the ice's surface and walked back and forth across it, never slipping, using the swirling fan for perfect balance.

The fan also swirled in the dining area and in the kitchen. There she learned of the animals. She made delicacies for the Hanshi and herself. She created works of culinary art from fish, toads, lizards, snakes, wasps, spiders, and bears, as well as other creatures. She learned which parts of the animals and insects not to use—the parts that were lethal poisons. She learned the same about plants.

In the spring and fall, she would dance. Oh, how she would dance. She would dance the ten walks: nuki ashi, the stealthy step; suri ashi, the rub step; shime ashi, the tight step; tobi ashi, the flying step; kata ashi, the one step; o ashi, the big step; ko ashi, the little step; kakizami, the small step, wari ashi, the proper step; and tsune ashi, the normal step.

The seasons went by in a swirl of creative ecstasy for Rhea. She did not stop dancing until she was a woman. Then she always was by the Hanshi's side. She learned the purpose of her life from him. She listened and understood her heritage. She was "kunoichi"; a creature who existed to serve the Hanshi, to be the Hanshi's servant in all things.

"*You* understand your duty," the Hanshi said, implying the treachery of Rhea's mother, who the Hanshi said had sold the sixteen-year-old into slavery after her failure at the tea ceremony. "But you do not understand yourself. You cannot serve me as the others can, but they cannot serve me as you can. It is genetically impossible. You cannot serve me as a warrior. You can only serve me as a woman. You know what you can do with your body. You must learn what you can do with your being."

Rhea accepted this as she accepted all Hanshi ways. Silently, with complete trust. The Hanshi had saved her from her mother's treachery. The Hanshi had given her life back. The Hanshi had never steered her wrong. In other words, the Hanshi worked—as her family, her country, and her religion never had.

She learned to sculpt her own face with cosmetics instead of carving an ice face with an icepick. She learned how to dress herself instead of dressing a food plate. The outward beauty filled her days. The inner beauty filled her nights. She explored herself, driving away the memories of the men who had assaulted her.

Each day she would spend in the Hanshi's dwelling. Each night she would return to her own to find another implement of pleasure on her bedding. Implement of pleasure is certainly a nice way of putting it. A nasty way of putting would be "sex aids." Rhea explored and extended her sexual power. She learned to control her needs and emotions. She exercised her vaginal muscles until they were as familiar to her as her arms or legs.

They tested her new-found strength, as they had tested her other abilities. But on a different sort of iceman this time. The Hanshi gave much to her, but he wanted much in return. She swore that she would give him what he wanted. On this day, in this winter season, he wanted her to go to a man.

She did not know whether the Hanshi knew the extent of what he was asking. She had not known a man since the rape. In the interim she had fallen in love with herself. She received his request with the only denial she was capable of: she did not accept silently.

"Do you want him to die?" she asked proudly.

"No," he said with a smile. "I want him to live."

"You don't want me to kill him?" she asked, echoes of the Yuki-onna in her voice.

"No," he repeated. "I want you to revive him."

That was all the Hanshi said. She returned to her dwelling to prepare the weapons for the night. There was a single ceramic mask on her bed mat. It was the painted face of a kind female spirit.

Rhea put on a luxurious silk robe and went to the man. Though she walked barefoot in the snow, she tracked no water on the dark wood floor of the dwelling.

She saw the dead man on his mat. His face was emotionally ravaged. His eyes glowed with the same intensity as the Snow Woman's. He too stood on a mountain of the dead. The wind buffeted his empty soul as well.

She kneeled before him and bowed. He placed a hand on her arm and then her knee. He looked at her without question or desire. She opened her robe and let it drop to the floor. He took her into his arms and drew her down to the mat.

On the first night he slept, holding her in his arms.

There were times when she felt like fighting his embrace; when panic and fear threatened to overwhelm her. But she felt his warmth, his need, his . . . tragedy. It was as real as his arms, this despairing tragedy. She could see the haunting of this man as if it were projected.

She felt his strong arms around her and lost all fear. This man had suffered worse than she. He was alien; with round eyes, a tall, strong body, and light brown hair. And his gray eyes gleamed with . . . something. Madness, she supposed. But they shone in the dark like beacons. She felt attracted to them, like a moth to the flame.

She had her assignment. The next night she soothed him. The following night they caressed each other. They slept together for the first time. That is, Rhea felt secure enough to sleep as well.

When the Hanshi saw her the next day, he felt impelled to tell her more. "I am pleased," he began. "You have done well."

"You have spoken to the man?" she asked demurely, head down, mimicking a professional geisha.

"No," the Hanshi replied. "I need not. I can see more on your faces than I could ever hear. Simply the fact that he has accepted you after what he has experienced speaks volumes."

"Excuse my impertinence, but I ask only to perform my duty better. What is it that he has experienced?"

The Hanshi smiled upon her. "You shall know soon enough," he promised. "And not from my lips. Go to him, for he is yours and you are his."

Rhea Tagashi never knew a greater excitement. Her body, her being, had betrayed her. Even the discovery of her own self-worth had not filled her with such elation. Her love was all the greater because it was love without reason.

That evening, she shuddered when he touched her. They made love.

Every night she would come to him and they would make love.

And, one night, he was gone. Rhea did not cry or run. She was kunoichi—what was, was. She lay on his bed and fell asleep.

She could block the despair and anguish, but not the sadness and loneliness. That too was clear to the Hanshi when he came to her days later. He was proud that she did not come to him. She knew that it would have been foolish as well as useless. She was, indeed, kunoichi.

"You must go to him," he said. She accepted that as she accepted all things, on the surface. But her heart knew the difference.

"Good," he nodded, noting her silent acceptance. "But you must go as my slave, not his."

She looked at him in confusion. "I serve you in all things," she maintained.

"You do not understand," the Hanshi said gravely. "If you joined him now, you would be as a child in the ways of society. You have lived within walls all your life. The walls of Ichi, the walls of Chiba. You must learn to live within the walls of the world. You must become *chitsumishi.*"

"Watch your fucking ass, will you, lady?"

They don't talk the same in the ninja school as they do on the streets of San Francisco.

PART THREE
KAPPA

Season of Lava,
Season of Sand,
Season of Woman,
Season of Man.
The Year of the Ninja Master

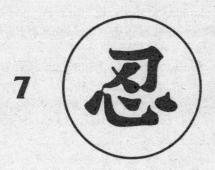

7

White and blue and brown and gold.

On this night, in this place, those were the world's only four colors.

The white of the snow that covered everything everywhere for as far as the eye could see and the mind imagine, the white of the half moon, and the white of the thin wisps of smoke coming from the chimney.

The blue of the moonlight that carpeted the snow—making it cool to the eye.

The brown of the wood, the trees, and the cabin.

The gold of the fire's glow that filled the interior of the house.

The house was a log cabin, nestled among the pine trees in a natural gulley. It looked peaceful under the vast, dark-blue night sky.

The pain came to him again. But, thank God, not through his brain.

He moved through the wood, through the snow that came up to his ankles. He moved silently even with the equipment on his back. He blended with the white of the snow and the blue of the night. He was a man in an all white suit, covering him from his head to his feet. Over his eyes was a dark-blue visor.

He moved quickly across the bumpy ground, across the cold carpet covering the forest's rocks and twigs and dead leaves. He moved low to the ground, his shape revealed every time he passed a tree. He moved directly toward the lone cabin.

Inside the cabin a man and woman lay side by side on a deep, comfortable sofa. The man had one arm on his love's distended stomach. There was no other arm.

The man in white approached the door of the house. He only stopped when a form erupted out of the snow in front of him.

A long, straight blade swept by his face as the man pivoted to one side. His hands were on the form's arms, his foot between the form's legs. He introduced the top of the form's head to a tree trunk.

There was a soft, sickeningly wet noise that blended with a sharp cracking sound. The tree shook. Snow was shaken from its branches. It fell onto the fallen form's back. But the man in white was no longer there.

He was at the side of the house, standing, his feet wide, in front of a window. Another form, with another sword, charged silently. The sword reached the man's nose, then jerked back as the form reached the man's suddenly outstretched leg.

The form fell heavily to the ground on his back. The man's arm moved up, then down. There was a coughing sound and the form moved no more. The man did.

He ran to the back of the house where another form was against the rear door. The man pointed at the form's head and there was another cough. The form's head jerked back and slapped against the door frame. Then it crumbled to the ground. The man kept moving.

He ran to the other side of the house. A form was running along a branch twenty feet in the air. He leaped off the branch, toward the cabin's roof. The man pointed at him and had a coughing fit. The form writhed in the air.

Only the sword reached the roof. It hit, and stuck in the sloping logs. The form fell toward the side wall, but the man leaped up and grabbed him by the ankle. With a yank, he brought them both down.

The man landed on his feet. The form was slammed down by his leg onto his face. It hardly made a difference. He was already dead.

Yasuru half sat, half lay next to Shika inside the warm cabin. He lay with his hand on her stomach. He felt the child kicking inside her. It was close. She would give birth soon.

The world outside made no difference to him now. All that mattered was her and the baby. They had traveled across the world to find this haven. In Maine, of all places. They had started their odyssey—their exodus—as soon as they discovered she was pregnant. Lord knew they had had enough sex between them to start a large family.

She used to be Rachel Assaf, but that name made no difference, or sense, anymore. No more than the name of Jeff Archer, which used to be his. Yasuru meant Archer in Japanese, as Shika meant Rachel (Rachel means "deer" in hebrew—Shika means "deer" in Japanese). Jeff and Rachel were names that lay across a huge gulf at the moment. Those were names that belonged to previous lives. As far as the world knew, both Jeff Archer and Rachel Assaf were dead. Those were their names before the Ninja Master.

The cabin door swung in. Shika gasped and grabbed the steel blue .357 revolver that lay between the sofa frame and the cushions. Yasuru vaulted over her to put himself between his love and the door.

A man in white stood framed in the doorway. He had gray eyes and close-cropped wheat-colored hair. He held a silenced MAC-11 machine pistol in his hand. A MAC-11 that was painted pure white.

"You know you've got a sword sticking out of your roof?" Daremo said, as he closed the door.

Archer couldn't believe his eyes. His eyes certainly gave that impression. They got larger and larger and his mouth dropped open. Shika just snorted, shook her head, and lowered the gun.

Archer ran forward, his one arm out. He suddenly stopped in front of the man. "All right?" he asked by way of permission, his right arm still out.

Daremo considered it for a second, then nodded.

The student embraced his master in joy. Daremo smiled, with honest pleasure. It was not the smile of a man who had just killed four others. It was the smile of a father finding his family. A family whose only profession was hunting. He patted Archer on the back, then moved inside.

"Nice entrance," Shika commented as Daremo came toward her, taking off his gloves.

"I'm known for them," he said, kneeling by her. "Whose is it?" he asked seriously, nodding his head toward her stomach.

"I don't know," she said flatly. "And I don't care." She looked him right in the eye as she said it. The father could only be one of two. He or Yasuru. Daremo sighed deeply. He had chosen her well. He thought she would survive the incredible upheaval of her life, and it appeared she had.

"You're all right now," Archer said without question as he pulled a thick wood chair from the table. He had reason to wonder. The last time he saw Daremo, the man had been a wreck.

"Well, I don't go through the tortures of the damned when I get near you anymore," Daremo said over his shoulder as his associate sat down.

"What the hell happened?" Shika asked. "And start from the beginning. I want to hear all of this."

These were not three human beings talking. They had gone beyond human emotions and human reactions. They lived in a world outside the world. No place on earth and none in heaven. But wherever they were, they intended to enjoy it as much as possible.

They had accepted their fates as "ki-chigaino": the walking crazy. They could not have possibly survived their experiences without becoming either a babbling, catatonic crazy, or ki-chigaino.

"I'll tell you as we go," Daremo said, standing up.

"Go?" Archer exclaimed. "Go where?"

"I'm here, aren't I?" Daremo replied cryptically.

"That means others are here as well," Archer surmised.

"We've got a sword stuck in our roof," Shika reminded him.

"Shit," quoth the Yasuru, looking at Shika's stomach. "Could we dig in here?" he asked his mentor.

"They would burn down the house," Shika said, getting up with Daremo's help. "We wouldn't have a chance."

"Best to get into a crowd," Daremo said.

"Couldn't they kill us just as easily there?" Archer asked helplessly.

Daremo shook his head. "Not anymore. There's been too much public killing. This is the worst possible place you could stay. If you remained here, they might be tempted to try again. But they've turned over El Salvador, Israel, and Hong Kong. So they can't afford any more public slaughters. Safety in numbers, don't you know."

"I don't understand," Archer complained. "Won't it be easy to kill us in an American city? We'll just be one of dozens weekly."

Daremo stilled, looking directly at his "jonin."

"The war is over," he said.

Both Shika and Archer stared at the Ninja Master.

Still the young man couldn't leave it alone. He had his love and her baby to consider.

"But, if the war is over...?" Yasuru started.

"There's still revenge," Daremo reminded him calmly. "There's been an extraordinary amount of death because this whole thing was too personal. That was and still is the opposition's fatal flaw. If they all weren't so intent on proving something to us, we would not have won."

"Won?" Shika said in amazement. "Won what?"

"This," said Daremo, smiling down at her.

That was enough. She had never seen this man before. She had seen the face of the man named Isaac Weisman, who had married her. She had seen the face of a Daremo who couldn't be near Rachel and Jeff when they were together without suffering terrible mental torture. The last time she had seen the face, it had been contorted in such pain that she shrank away from it, terrified and crying.

It kept her silent and somewhat content as they left Maine. Daremo was prepared. Not for them, trekking across the countryside like three desperate escapees from a Gulag in Siberia. Daremo had a white MAC-11 and he had a brown four-wheel-drive RV.

When Shika fell asleep between the two men, Archer asked Daremo about their chances.

"They'll be no ninjas on the highway tonight," Daremo assured him. "For the moment, we're in the real world. The four at the cabin were a wild shot. They were put on your trail as soon as things fell apart in Bar Sinai. It

took them this long to find you. They were alone, with
no backup."

"How can you be so sure? Were you following them
the whole time?"

Daremo shook his head, keeping his eyes on the road
and his hands on the wheel. "I was busy elsewhere. But
where I was busy, they were busy."

"Who's they? Ninja? Moshuh Nanren?"

"Both."

They sat silently for a time while the vehicle crossed
into Massachusetts.

"It doesn't work," Archer suddenly said.

"No," Daremo said with a smile. "It doesn't."

"What the hell happened, Brett?"

Daremo smiled again. He had come a very long way.
He had come through five hells and survived. He had
suffered losses and gains beyond any normal person's
comprehension. He had lost families, lives, and abilities.
Archer had tried to send a mental message to him just
then and had hit a brick brain wall.

"I don't want to repeat the story twice," he said,
nodding toward the sleeping girl.

Archer clamped his mouth shut in frustration. But
not for long. "If you're here, where are they?"

It was a good question, so Daremo answered it.
"Japan."

"If they're there," Archer immediately responded,
"why are you here?"

"I decided," Daremo said simply, watching the road,
"that if I let this baby die, I didn't deserve to live."

Archer looked across at his master in reverence and

shock. He couldn't conceive of anything to say for a few minutes. He kept stumbling across the incredible happenings of their lives in his mind. He thought until the memories overwhelmed his understanding. "Will this ever end?" he asked helplessly.

Daremo looked out the windshield at the country road lined with the army of his dead.

"No," he said.

They left the RV in Hartford and took a plane west, picking up a car when they landed. They went cross-country to a place both Archer and Daremo knew very well. They both seemed to gravitate to the place where it had started.

Daremo drove through the Mission District, past a street where a martial arts studio once stood. In its place was a religious mission and a pizza parlor. He drove through Japantown, one of two Oriental sections of the city—past a block where a restaurant once did business. A drugstore and an insurance office were where it used to be.

He drove until they left the city, over the Golden Gate bridge, heading north. They passed Sausalito, traveling on a street where a townhouse still stood. It looked the same from the outside. The only difference was that Brett Wallace didn't live there anymore. Daremo kept driving, but he remembered. He remembered it all.

They passed Vista Point, offering the expectant mother a glorious view of the bay area. Now this was more like it. They were getting away from it all again.

Daremo drove up Route 101 until they reached Sonoma County. They stopped in a small crossroads town and rented a two-story frame house. There they waited for Shika to give birth. While they waited, they told stories to each other: ridiculous stories; unbelievable stories; stories that tested their own credulity as they told them; true stories.

"Rachel Assaf is dead," the woman suddenly exclaimed, her contractions coming closer together. "And her husband, Isaac Weisman, never really existed."

"Well," Daremo said in an upper register, moving his palm in a "maybe so-maybe not" motion.

"The Isaac Weisman I knew never existed," she countered. He nodded. "So I really don't have a last name." She mused. "I like Shika, but I like Rachel too. From now on I'm Rachel Shika."

"Done!" Archer announced, holding her hand as she lay on the bed.

"The baby really should have a last name," she concluded.

"The baby really should have a first name," Archer said.

"First, I mean, last things first," she replied, intent on her stomach.

"Are you sure about this?" Archer asked Daremo—unnecessarily.

"I've sent too many out," he replied flatly, "I can bring one in."

Rachel began to feel serious pain. "Tell me a story," she gasped, sweat collecting on her forehead and neck. "From the beginning."

"Once upon a time," Daremo said, as he went about the business of delivering her baby. "There lived a man named Brian Williams. He was born in Columbus Ohio in 1945. His father was a successful real-estate speculator and his mother was a housewife.

"When he was seven he took his first self-defense class at the local YMCA. When he was twelve he started taking karate classes at a studio near the campus of Ohio State University.

"At the age of eighteen, he was admitted to O.S.U. as a philosophy major, where he discovered the parallel wonders of meditation. From his friends, he discovered there's more to the martial arts world than judo, karate, and jujitsu. He discovered, hell, there was more to jujitsu, karate, and judo than just chop-chop, kick-kick, and throw-throw.

"His passion for all forms of self-defense and self-discovery kept him busy throughout his cushy college career. It also kept him away from drugs, booze, and cigarettes.

"'I'm high on life, man,' he'd say while everybody around him barfed.

"Everybody around him peeled off too. After a few months or a few years, everybody else in his Midwest sphere got what they wanted out of spiritualism or got tired of it. They went on to other things, like the legal system or business. After a while they found Brian's continued devotion to self-improvement and breaking things with various parts of his body irritating at worst and troubling at best.

"When he went to India to study with a Tibetan monk

in 1966, most everyone figured that was it. They saw it as his attempt to be hopelessly hip. They bought meditation the same way they bought swamp land in Florida. About the only friend he had left was Alex Redman, who had followed his muse to a university in Tokyo, which just so happened to need a good Tibetan meditation teacher.

"Williams escaped the hysteria on American campuses to live with Redman in Japan. There Alex introduced him to a very nice Japanese student named Kyoko Susuki who was very interested in Western philosophy and became very interested in Williams's bod. Thankfully the feeling was mutual, and the mutual feeling resulted in matrimony.

"'Come home, son, all is forgiven,' his father writes. A lucrative job in real estate awaits.

"'Oh, boy, pop,' Williams writes back. 'I need lots of the long green stuff to keep my family in the manner we will become accustomed to. But first I have to go visit a ninja training camp.'"

"What?" Archer interrupted.

"Keep your mind on business," Daremo said.

"That's right. Mas Yamaguchi introduced himself to Williams at a martial arts show and was so impressed by the Occidental's skill and integrity that he drove him to the really hush-hush ninja training ground in Chiba, outside Tokyo."

"What?" Archer repeated, unable to believe his ears.

"That's how it happened!" Daremo almost shouted. Rachel almost shouted with him.

"He just *showed* you the ninja camp? Just like that?" Archer asked incredulously.

"Just like that," Daremo grunted. "On the first date and everything.

"His only reason seemed to be to discuss the pros and cons of such an organization, an organization Yamaguchi swore was based on spiritual as well as physical disciplines.

"'They're terrorists,' Williams said.

"'They're warriors,' Yamaguchi corrected.

"'They work for money,' the roundeye countered.

"'They work for causes,' the slanteye promised.

"'No matter what the situation,' Brian had said loftily, 'barring immediate self-defense of myself or my family, I don't feel that I could use my martial arts discipline to cause pain to others.'

"Yamaguchi, in a magnificent show of restraint, did not barf. Instead, he spoke of karma and yin-yang, and all sorts of things that made the whole she-bop sound like 'Aw, I was just kidding, roundeye. Let's pretend I never even mentioned a school to learn the deadliest art of assassination known.'

"He was way before his time," Daremo said between breaths (his own and Rachel's). "He ladled it all on; ninjutsu as a spiritual art."

Archer didn't say anything, but the expression on his face as he helped Rachel breathe properly gave a hint of the derision he felt for such cockamamy concepts.

"Brian liked the guy, though," Daremo said quietly. "Brian thought he was one hell of a guy.

"Now the fun part. The part where Brian Williams

comes back to the United States with his beautiful Oriental wife, to be welcomed with open arms by his totally understanding, totally charitable, totally supportive family.

"They give him a beautiful job in his dad's beautiful business and they give her a beautiful condo outside beautiful Columbus, and they give them both a big beautiful welcome home party. One year later and the fairy tale continues. Brian loves his job and loves his life and loves his wife so well that she's pregnant.

"His parents are so darn pleased that they decide to throw a dinner party for the happy couple. So they invite ten of their dearest friends who bring their dates and everybody has such a swell time that Brian has to drive some of the soused well-wishers home.

"That's who Brian should have killed," Daremo murmured.

"He comes home a half hour later and finds everyone dead. Not just dead—slaughtered. Butchered with a vengeance. Mom and Dad have been dismembered. The wife has been raped repeatedly before and after her demise."

"Daremo . . ." Yasuru cautioned.

"I want to hear it," Rachel pushed through clenched teeth. "I want to hear it all."

Daremo let the irony wash all over him. He lost that child. He would not lose this one.

"The alleged perpetrators are caught in record time. Three real thrill-seeking publicity hounds. The papers termed them 'three young men in their middle twenties who are believed to be members of a notorious motorcycle gang.' The reports went on to suggest that 'the police believe that the alleged perpetrators may have been under the influence of the drug PCP, a substance better known to the public as angel dust.'

"A trial date is set. A jury is chosen. The arguments for the defense and prosecution start. And guess what? The case is thrown out of court on a technicality. I won't tell you which one. Does it make any difference? The three confessed killers are let go because they have to be. No freedom, no story.

"The next part's really good. To everyone's surprise, Brian Williams decides to kill the trio, then get out of town. He lures the guys to a secluded rendezvous, then rearranges the formats of their faces. In slow motion and with great special effects, he gouges eyes, breaks necks, kicks open a head, and actually rips a guy's heart out. How symbolic. How subtle.

"It's Brian's turn to barf. Afterward, he goes directly to Tokyo. He goes to Mas Yamaguchi and confesses his sins.

"'Can I be a ninja now? Huh? Can I, can I, oh please, can I?'

"'Sure, kid. Follow me! We're off to see the wizard, the wonderful wizard of Oz!'

"I love happy endings, don't you?" Daremo inquired.

Archer stared at his sensei—disbelief rendering him mute. Or maybe it was understanding. At long last, understanding. Actually, his silence was due to a little of both. He had heard this story before, but not this way. This way he had to think about it.

"But the story wasn't over yet. Brian changed his

name to Brett Wallace and studied ninjutsu for a full
decade. And once he had proved himself, this tip-top
secret Oriental organization let him leave. Let him walk
away . . . just like that. They didn't give him an assignment; he gave himself one—in his own words, 'to help
others as wronged as myself.' What a guy.

"Within a year of going back to the United States and
moving to Sausalito, Brett Wallace had a nifty bachelor
pad, a Japanese restaurant, and some sort of be-all,
catch-all kungfu dojo."

"What about the money?" Rachel grunted. "Where
did he get the money?"

"He took his dad's cash and deposited it all over the
place under false names, let it accrue interest for ten
years, and then reclaimed it. It made for quite a
bankroll. So he had the cash and with a name dropped
by Yamaguchi, he had an automatic squeeze—another
beautiful Oriental girl named Rhea Tagashi. Amazing
how things fall right in place for this bozoid, isn't it?

"A nice girl, this Rhea. Very considerate, very affec-
tionate, very good in bed. Really made Brett feel at
home. She didn't work alone, though. She had this cook
named Hama backing up her song and dance. Together
they went right along with Brett's idea to become the
Lone Ranger.

"His first mission, since he decided to accept it, was
to save the ass of this snotty-nosed kid named Jeff
Archer and wipe the asses of a street gang who had
raped and immolated the kid's grandma. From then on,
it was Batman and Robin time—with the reverential

sidekick supplying comedy relief whenever anything got too subtle."

"I don't know," Archer said worriedly, looking at Rachel's straining face and the blood on the bed. "Could you do a Cesarian?"

Daremo looked at him in disbelief until Archer looked back at him. Then they both broke up.

Could he do a Cesarian? Archer had seen the man peel a grape with a samurai sword!

"What . . . happened . . . then?" Rachel gasped.

"Brett Wallace died and was reborn," Daremo told her. "To put it bluntly, Brett Wallace was an asshole who did everything he could to blow his cover. Instead of being a ninja, he was acting like millionaire playboy Bruce Wayne. He drank like a fish, he was a gourmet cook, he frequented all the posh places, and he slept around. Yamaguchi had to come to America and ream his ass—following was two years of 'retraining.'"

"Retraining . . ." Archer echoed. He knew what that meant. Undiluted, condensed torture. There was no trouble telling whether a student of ninja retraining had graduated. If he was alive, he had passed.

"The new, improved Brett Wallace came back to the West Coast a better person. Brett Wallace came back the avenger of the meek and the assassin of the strong.

"Brett Wallace lived for three years," Daremo said. But the next few minutes were taken up with renewed activity between Rachel's legs, so he never got a chance to tell her about all the wonderful things the new and improved Brett Wallace did.

He never did get to tell her about the three years of

nonstop killing. About the people he had sliced open, and how they looked when they died and how the blood had spurted and how they had soiled themselves and the disgusting smells and the screams.

"What then?" she asked when nothing came of the last contraction. Anything to get her mind off the labor.

"I'd like to think that Brett Wallace became sane," Daremo said, almost wistfully. "But Brett Wallace went nuts."

"It was the Chinese psychic attack," Archer said in his defense.

"That anything like the Chinese water torture?" Rachel grimaced.

"Close," Daremo admitted. "Brett Wallace went nuts and then died. The Figure in Black showed up for the first time, plunging gold needles into Wallace and the arm Jeff Archer used to have. The needles gave Archer a degenerative nerve disease. The needles plunged Brett into a coma from which he never recovered. Waking up instead was Daremo.

"And Daremo made his stolen fortune, then went to Central America because that was where the Figure led. Daremo was still just a newborn, with the tortures of the damned inside his head. So at first he sought relief. But then he sought the reason for his existence."

Rachel almost barfed this time. What stopped her was the knowledge of what she herself had gone through.

"In an El Salvador terrorist training camp funded by the Chinese, there was a Central American shaman, who somehow concentrated Archer's disease in his left arm and relieved Daremo's mental agony. But when the curtain of anguish left him, he only got a glimpse of what was beneath.

"He followed where the Figure in Black led. As did Archer. As did Brett Wallace's friends—who sought to take vengeance on Brett Wallace's killer."

Rachel wanted to speak. But she couldn't. Nature, at its most wondrous, called. All she could do was push and try to keep breathing.

"The trail led to Israel, where a woman named Rachel Assaf was married to a man named Isaac Weisman. She was a police officer. He was a security man at a nuclear missile installation. Only he had died several years prior and she was being assailed by psychic tortures—not to mention real life tortures. It seemed as if the entire country was going mad, and she with it.

"Members of the Israeli mafia died while babbling biblical quotes. Others died whispering words from the Koran. A faceless Arab terrorist was stalking her. Members of her own internal security forces were kidnapping and interrogating her.

"She escaped to a man named Yasuru. A man with a dead left arm. And to both their wonders, they could mentally communicate with each other. Their minds were opened by powers Daremo had acquired from the psychic attacks. In the Negev desert they discovered the kunoichi and the yamabushi intent on carrying out the death sentence handed down by the Hanshi.

"They also discovered the Figure in Black and the Faceless One in a missile silo. The latter was eager to detonate the bomb. The former was eager to kill the latter. The truth emerged—the Chinese sought to paralyze the American and Israeli espionage communities with diversions. Diversions for what? The answer lay in China.

"Daremo was now two men. One was the calculating ninja. The other was a terrified child, unable to deal with his broadened mental abilities. The mind is too complex for even its owner to understand. The Chinese psychic assault had opened up Daremo's mental powers. And he was rapidly losing control.

"No more fairy tales," Daremo told her as she struggled to keep understanding. "Pure science fantasy now."

"I took a man whose life was over and I made him me. I pushed his own memories into his subconscious and filled his conscious with my memories. For all intents and purposes he *was* me. But he was also my diversion. While he claimed Huangshan Mountain from the front, I climbed it from the rear. While he confronted the psychic assaulter, I waited in ambush.

"It was the mystic Hui," Daremo said in a monotone. "He had accidentally extended his own consciousness and attacked me without knowing that his attack would automatically extend mine. But neither of us knew what had actually happened. Neither of us could completely control the abilities.

"But they experimented. Experimented until Hui could no longer live among normal people. He could not communicate on a physical level anymore. He had developed the mother Messianic complex of them all.

"He said—or something akin to saying—that the Chinese magician spies, the Moshuh Nanren, were responsible for the security on a project to return China to the Cultural Revolution."

"Time travel?" Archer asked incredulously.

After all this, Daremo wouldn't have put it past them. But he said, "I doubt it."

"It was something all too real. But Daremo still did not know what that was. All he knew—all he could get from Hui's mind—was the fact that the Plan was postponed.

"That was all, because Hui was dead. All of him. After we defeated the Moshuh Nanren in El Salvador and Israel, the people responsible for the Plan decided it was too risky to continue."

"But what was the Plan?" Archer complained. He had a perfect right to. He had lost his left arm to it.

"It had to be a worldwide assault. Or else the M-Ns wouldn't have been trying to distract the American and Israeli forces."

They all thought, or tried to. Soon the birth plan took precedence. Daremo didn't get to tell them how his final battle with Hui eliminated the extra powers in his mind. It was too farfetched, in any event.

He didn't have to tell them how he returned to this country to find them. He didn't have to start telling them why it was important. He didn't have to explain to them why it was even necessary. Yet.

He didn't have to say that the ninja and the Moshuh Nanren were still out there. He didn't have to tell them that Rhea and Hama were still out there. He didn't have to tell them that the Figure in Black was still out there.

And that they all wanted Daremo, Yasuru, and Shika dead.

And why.

Daremo had a terrible feeling he knew.

A short time later there was a fourth person that the others would want dead.

8

Their laughter filled the house. Their faces were sweaty, their limbs exhausted. Their joy was overwhelming and nearly hysterical. There was an edge to their celebration of life.

It was just a small respite—a tiny oasis—from the madness their existence had become. But it was all they had. And it had to do.

They laughed and laughed and laughed.

Their laughter and their flushed, delight-twisted faces faded into pure white light. The pure white of wisping clouds set in a clear, bright-blue sky surrounded a full sun, a blazing sun lighting the cold white ground. The smooth, uninterrupted snow encircled the Maine log cabin. Its untouched powder stretched off in all directions.

The man and woman trudged across the nature-rich environment. Their movements were accompanied by no sound. No white gauze appeared at their lips or nostrils as they breathed the cold air. They did not appear to be breathing at all, if frozen exhalations or movement of their chests were any evidence.

No sound could be heard, but their emotions could be sensed by their angry expressions. It was hard to decide which was the more intense. The man was as tall as the woman, but much wider. He wore all white: baggy white pants, a burly white coat. His boots were white.

The only thing that set off the purity of the color was the livid red line that crossed between his eyes, over the bridge of his nose, and ended on his right cheek. It accompanied the strange red-lined groove in his forehead. He walked with the help of an eight-foot-long, jade-green pole. Bouncing against his thigh as he went was a strange, oval device with a handle and trigger-button—which was attached to his belt.

The woman wore a white and brown camouflage design across her turtleneck top and ankle-tied pants. Her boots were also white. In her hand was a sleek chestnut-brown automatic weapon—a silenced 9mm Heckler and Koch HK4. The beauty of her face was twisted by her expression of pained determination.

Her eyes were delicately almond-shaped, their blackness deep and lustrous. Her skin was off-white and smooth. Her rich black hair was cut short.

The pair walked side by side toward the quiet cabin. They had searched for it during many frustrating weeks. Prior months had been consumed by recuperation. They had to survive the scars that were left on his face and across her now-covered torso. They had let others do their work then, but returned to the field when the others were not heard from.

The quarry had not been traced, but their hunters had been. The man's pace slowed deliberately until he stopped. The woman stopped as well, looking to him. He pointed with the snow-covered bottom end of his stick. Her eyes went to where he pointed. Before them, between them and the cabin, were two mounds of snow—like so many other mounds they had passed or walked across.

She raised her gun. His stick was there to lower her arm. He carefully, gingerly prevented her from taking aim at the shapes. He looked at her once, then suddenly danced silently forward, his knees bending completely, his feet high above the ground.

He was "yoko-aruki"—side-walking across the top of the snow. The footprints left in the snow went in both directions and not a stream of disrupted powder was left as a clue to which way the man had gone.

His staff was high over his head, protecting him from possible overhead ambush. Just as he approached the first mound, the staff stabbed down, deep into the snow. He jammed it into the shape like a pike. He planted his feet and jerked the pole up. Erupting from the snow cover was a figure. As it flew into the air in a cloud of snow and dirt, the woman crouched and fired—the nine-millimeter slug punching the form high in the chest.

As the first figure fell backward the man jammed the pole into the second mound, repeating the action. The woman was tense and calm at the same time. Her eyes narrowed and she shot the second figure in the forehead, dotting the snow behind the flying form with red sleet. The second form spun backward and crashed back to the ground on its shoulders.

The man stood between the fallen bodies, the anger on his face remaining. He did not look at the woman or the figures. He stared at the snow a few feet ahead of him as the woman neared. She looked at the two dead men.

They had died twice. They had already been dead when buried in the snow. They had Oriental faces; the faces of two out of four that had been sent in the man and woman's place. In the pits from which the man had torn them were two more bodies. They had been buried on top of each other.

Rhea almost snarled, lowering her gun. Hama held up a quieting hand. He quickly pointed at another two mounds in the snow off to the right of the cabin. He started moving quickly in that direction, but stopped dead in his tracks as soon as Rhea followed. He tried to turn back the way he had come, but it was too late.

The second two corpses in the shallow grave behind them erupted from the earth under their own power.

The first charged forward, past Rhea. She raised the gun, but just as it squared with the corpse's back, it was out of her hand, stinging her fingers. The gun whipped through the air, then slammed into a tree trunk. It stuck there, pinned by a hook through its trigger guard. The hook was attached to a jointed chain. The chain stretched behind her, then fell lax.

She saw Hama out of the corner of her eye as she whirled. The first "corpse" had jumped toward him. The figure led with its left arm, which Hama smashed with his pole. The arm fell off... into the corpse's right hand. It slipped from its sleeve and the corpse used the thin, straight, metal arm as a weapon.

She heard the first clash of metal against metal as another pair of arms wrapped around her, pinning her own arms to her waist. She had been planning to use her legs to kick at the other corpse, but her feet were already off the ground. The corpse threw her to the snow face first. It didn't tackle or trip her. It threw her... hard.

There was no chance to spin or roll. The strong arms slammed her to the ground. She moved her hands to push herself up or away, but the muscles wouldn't respond. Her elbows were cinched together by a loop of some strong, thin material. It would have been painful if she hadn't been so agile and strong.

So strong, in fact, that when her upper body would not leave the ground, she chopped and windmilled her legs, spinning her shape off the snow. Her legs bent, her feet aiming for the earth. Another leg, not her own, swept across her calves, knocking her feet toward the sky.

She let their dive carry her head toward the ground, then continued the spin so she somersaulted backward in mid-air. She landed and kicked, but it was already too late. A forearm hit her across the chest, between her breasts and her neck—driving her back and, originally, down.

She back-somersaulted again, increasing her speed, then did it again, trying to get out of range of the corpse. It was no good. It was right alongside as she went. She stopped, spinning out instead of backward, hoping to knock it down with her knees.

Instead, it caught her knees between its body and arm. It let her torso wrap perpendicular to its, then snapped her back the way she had come. Her legs scissored out, but without the balance of her now-tied arms, it was hopeless. She fell stomach first to the snow, her bent legs taking most of the brunt.

Hama and the other corpse jousted. They had a "sword fight" with the poles. Hama needed both hands to fully control his heavy "bo." The corpse's was shorter and thinner around, giving it more mobility. Naturally its handicap was its one arm. The empty left sleeve swirled with every turn, jerked with every thrust.

When he wasn't watching the short, dark silver weapon, Hama watched that sleeve. It gave more witness to the corpse's next move than the form's grinning face. Even so, Hama could not penetrate its defense. The display of control was dazzling...even better than their last meeting. It was as if the skill and energy of its left arm had flowed into its right at that distant moment of amputation.

They fought each other to a standoff. Hama changed the odds as he fought toward the tree where Rhea's gun was stuck. His adversary saw the strategy and joined him; the two making a parallel trek toward the gun.

Rhea saw what Hama was trying to do as her head and legs came up. Her big mistake was keeping her legs together too long. As they just started to separate, the corpse caught them both. Then they were corded about the knees the same way her elbows were caught. The corpse wrapped his arms around her ankles, kneeled, and held her legs and waist off the ground. Her chest and chin were pushed into the snow.

Hama put his plan into effect. He smashed at the other pole, preparing to fight with just one arm so he could reach the gun with his other.

The two were near the tree now. Hama reached. The corpse kicked. The foot knocked the hand away. Hama switched stances, reaching again. Another joint-tearing kick. The yamabushi's hand was knocked away. Hama immediately went back to fighting with both hands. He swung the pole in a vicious arc. The corpse nimbly ducked under it and smashed his pole against the gun broadside.

The pole bent the metal and broke the plastic. Hama stabbed his weapon forward, its round tip speeding toward the corpse's undefended middle. The corpse twisted and shot a kick around. Hama's pole scraped across the corpse's chest, tearing the dark cloth and skin beneath.

The corpse swung his metal stick back. Hama ducked beneath it and put all his strength into swinging his pole into the corpse's chest. The corpse bent backward, the stick sliding over his head. He spun backward, his feet going over Hama's pole. Hama jabbed up but met the corpse's stick which was laid across the corpse's chest.

The momentum spun the corpse around twice. He

landed on his feet, but crouched as the blunt end of Hama's stick stabbed at him again. His own arm thrust— not toward Hama, but the device Hama had on his belt.

As soon as the metal touched, Hama leaped back. His back touched another stick and he leaped forward.

He jerked in place, twisted, and retreated—his back to the cabin door.

He looked to his left. Yasuru stood there, metal "arm" in hand.

He looked to his right. Daremo stood there, his sheathed ten-foot-tall stick in his hand. The stick with his katana, wakizashi, and tanto secured inside—on either end. Beyond Daremo was the woman, trussed like a Purdue chicken in the snow.

Hama looked at them in disbelief. He opened his mouth, but no sound emerged.

"You are insane" both Daremo and Yasuru heard. They were Hama's words, but they came from Rhea's mouth.

Daremo didn't turn. Yasuru could see her from where he stood.

"Why?" Daremo replied quietly, earnestly. His eyes were still intent on Hama's silent visage, but he was speaking to them both. "What did we do that was so unusual? Weren't you taught to wait—silent, motionless— no matter what the conditions? Didn't you hang for hours from a tree? Maybe a day? Maybe many days?" Hama remembered, but said nothing. Daremo went on.

"Didn't you wait for hours in a pit you had dug in the frozen ground or the hot mud? Didn't you learn to

escape your hunters by swimming through their la-
trine? Didn't you spend hours in rivers of excrement?"

Hama looked away from the questions. He looked to
Yasuru's smiling face, his pole still at the ready. "It's the
way of ninja," the young man said.

"What now?" Rhea yelled, her face a half-inch off the
dirty snow.

Her question was well taken. It wasn't a Mexican
standoff. The Orientals were at a disadvantage. Hama
couldn't defeat the Ninja Master and the jonin at the
same time. And Rhea couldn't escape the tight bonds at
her elbows or knees, even by dislocating her joints. In
her situation, she could hardly stand. And even if she
could, she'd be practically useless to the warrior-priest.

Daremo's "indeed" was unspoken. "Let's go inside,"
he suggested, watching Hama.

"No!" Rhea barked. Her strong disagreement only
seemed to make Daremo calmer. "Let's go inside anyway," he said quietly.

Hama stared without expression for a second, then
turned and marched toward the cabin door. Daremo
moved backward until he was beside Rhea. He took her
by the elbows to stand her up. For a moment they
could look closely into each other's faces. Emotions,
like passing shadows, were swept off their visages as
their eyes met. Neither allowed any definite expression
to be seen.

Daremo lifted her easily, putting her across his shoul-
der. He went to the cabin before Yasuru, ready to use
Rhea as a weapon, if necessary. When they entered,
Hama redirected his attention to the renegade ninja.

Daremo seemed to ignore him. He threw Rhea onto the bed. She landed in a sitting position, bouncing once. She struggled against the bonds instinctively, but stopped as the rest of her stilled.

Daremo walked away from her. He went to one side of the room. Yasuru stood across from him, on the other side.

The Ninja Master looked at his once-trusted friend and advisor. His face was serious, even grave, but only at first. Then his entire body seemed to sigh. He didn't so much smile as grow weary. His face relaxed into something between a grin and resignation.

"I can't read your mind, you know," he said mildly. Hama did not react. "There's nothing in here that will destroy the house, and all of us with it." Still no reaction from the bald Japanese. "I know what I would have done," Daremo continued, the words all but flowing over each other in a hypnotic monotone. "If I had known we would be here. I would have attached explosives to myself. I would have died killing you."

He looked directly at Hama. "But I am counting on the fact that you will not commit suicide killing me. That, in this case—here, now—you will not commit suicide *trying* to kill me. You will not throw your life away."

The emotion was powerful in the room, oppressive. It was betrayal, regret, agony, loathing. Hama tried to ignore it.

"What do you want?" Rhea almost shrieked, her body straining forward with each word.

Daremo seemed to notice her for the first time, his

face a bland mask. "Turn to the side. I'll untie you."
She didn't move. She just stared at him. "Come on," he
urged. "Let me show off."

She turned to the side, giving herself the chance to
look away from him. His arm immediately whipped
forward, a dark blur. No one could clearly see what left
his hand, but they could hear the abrupt, angry buzz.
Rhea's elbows suddenly separated with a snap. The
shuriken went on to completely bury itself in the rear
wall.

A dull blue star with sharpened edges emerged from
the outside back wall. It spun like a Frisbee for many
feet then disappeared into the snow.

Rhea felt the power and pent-up energy in the star's
passing. She quickly reached down to undo her bound
knees.

They were all duly impressed. Not only had his
throw been powerful and precise, but no one could see
where the shuriken had come from. No one had spied
it in his belt or up his sleeve.

And not one of them bothered with any additional
artifice. There was no "How can you be sure we're
alone out here" from any party. It was as if they could,
indeed, read each other's minds. They had all been
trained in the Way. They had lived with each other for
years.

Daremo turned back to Hama as if expecting something. Derision, disrespect, a show of being unimpress-
ed . . . anything. Hama simply waited and watched.
Daremo redirected his attention.

"It's been a long time," he told Rhea without

import ... simply a statement of fact. "Since Central America." He looked absently at Yasuru, who viewed his sensei with concern.

"Three years," the one-armed man said.

"Three seasons," Daremo corrected vacantly, not looking at anything in particular.

"We've met since then," Yasuru continued a bit self-consciously, meaning to give Daremo time to collect what seemed to be his unraveling thoughts.

They had, after all, tracked Hama and Rhea, certain the two would find the Maine hideout. They had gone ahead and waited, buried beneath the corpses, the snow, and the dirt, motionless, for hours.

"In Bar Sinai," Yasuru reminded his adversaries.

Daremo's head snapped toward Hama. The Oriental was moving. He was slowly taking the device from his belt. He carefully wedged it against his neck and pressed the button. The voice that emerged from Hama's barely open mouth was metallic, robotlike.

"We remember," it said.

Yasuru remembered too. He remembered his sword between Hama's two hands, the blade just cutting the skin of Hama's scalp. He remembered his dead arm swinging around, powered by muscles in his shoulders and chest. He remembered the limb, bleeding black blood, propelling his stiff, lifeless fingers into Hama's ear. He remembered slicing his good hand down and knifing his fingers into Hama's throat.

Hama's throat.

He remembered Hama's throat giving way beneath the "iron palm" technique. He could feel the larynx being crushed beneath his hand even now.

"I made you a promise three seasons ago," Daremo told the yamabushi. "Even though you were not conscious to hear it. I said your time would come." He looked between the two, looking at neither, but seeing them both. "It has come. It is now."

The portentous pronouncement hung awkwardly in the morning air, in the sunlit room.

"So?" Hama's metallic voice, aided by the artificial voice box, grated.

"You must choose," Daremo said.

The two couldn't speak for another moment because they were too astonished.

"Haven't we made our positions clear?" Rhea almost stammered. "Isn't our choice apparent?" Even Yasuru looked to the sandy-haired man in confusion.

"That was then," Daremo pronounced. "This is now."

Hama threw his hands in the air and turned in place. He returned to an incredulous posture, staring at Daremo with impatience.

Daremo only smiled, letting the grin grow across his face, as if he were a mischievous child who had just proved a prank. He even allowed himself a small chuckle. "How else can I say it?" he asked helplessly. "There it is. As stupid as it sounds, there it is."

"There *what* is?" Rhea asked impatiently.

Daremo shook his head and shrugged. "I'm thinking cosmically. You're obviously still thinking about this realistically, though I don't see how." Hama and Rhea's face still showed blank hopelessness. "Now you're not thinking at all," Daremo suddenly said harshly. "Look at your faces! Closed shop!"

"Brett," Rhea interrupted angrily, "what do you want?"

"Brett is dead," Daremo said sullenly, looking at the floor.

"That won't help you," Rhea countered, just as angry as before. He looked at her sharply. "If you think pronouncing Brett Wallace dead will protect you, you're crazy."

"You're repeating yourself," Daremo said flatly.

Rhea stood up and started fearlessly toward the door.

"What was your mission?" Daremo asked quietly as she passed. That stopped her. But she had an answer.

"To kill you!" she said, turning on him. They faced each other. Yasuru kept his eyes on Hama, who seemed to be looking nowhere and everywhere at once.

"That is your mission," Daremo said, looking directly into her eyes. She could see no madness there. "Now. What was your mission?"

Rhea had to look away. She was starting to feel something she didn't want to feel. She looked down, shaking her head irritably. "What are you talking about?" She knew the next word would be a mistake, but she couldn't keep from saying it. "When?"

Daremo didn't smile, even though they both knew that was the magic word. "Six years ago," he said.

She didn't answer. But he could see her thinking. He could see that she was trying to understand now. Or, at least, she was realizing there was something to understand.

"Were you not assigned to me?" he continued mildly, his voice firm. "Are you not chitsumishi?"

Rhea visibly started. She had not heard that word in eleven years.

She looked to the man she loved more than she had ever loved anything, with a love more powerful than she could start to understand. Rhea Tagashi trembled.

Shiban Kan Hama seemed to move without moving. It was as if his brain had commanded his body to move, then immediately rescinded the order. He wavered, almost going out of focus. But he didn't move. A fleeting image went through his mind. If he moved, he would have been struck down by lightning coming from Daremo's brain.

Yasuru watched him carefully.

"Were you not a ninja sent to aid another infiltrating?" Daremo asked her softly. He waited. She nodded. "What was your mission here?"

She could not answer. She did not know.

Daremo looked over her shoulder. "What was *your* mission here?" he asked Hama. But then he waved a hand at the bald Oriental, as if dismissing him. "I know. Yamabushi. You were here to watch over me. To sit in judgment."

He looked back at the woman. "But not you. You are not a warrior-priestess. You are kunoichi. A woman ninja. A ninja always has an assignment, a duty to carry out. Rhea. What was your mission here?"

"To . . ." she faltered. "To help you."

"To help me what?"

"To help you . . . accomplish your desires."

She remembered the words. " 'He is yours and you are his. You must go to him.' "

"To help me punish evil?" Daremo snapped.

"Whatever you desired."

"To help me correct injustice?"

"Whatever you desired." She spoke as a hypnotised subject.

"Why?" he demanded. She blinked. "Why?" he asked the others as well as her. He moved away from her, toward the bed. His back was to her, but she could make no move to attack him.

He turned back before Hama could have accused her of dereliction of duty. "Why?" he asked again, this time directly at Hama. "Why did the Hanshi want you to help me do whatever I wanted to do? The Hanshi did not order *me* to do anything! I was accepted, I was trained, and I was released, free to go, from the most secretive organization in the world. With no orders! There has to be a reason."

Daremo looked at his hands. His back was bent, he moved nervously near the bed. "Of what possible purpose could I be to the ninja? Why did they let me in? Why did they train me? Not once, but twice! Why did they let me come back here?"

"It makes no difference." Hama's digitalized voice cut through the clear air like a hacksaw blade.

"*Of course* it makes a difference!" Daremo whirled on him. He moved two steps toward the Oriental and anchored his feet. "Of course it does. Are you that blind? That trusting?" Daremo's tone became mocking. "Or do you refuse to question because to question would destroy what sanity you have left?"

"Brett," Rhea groaned miserably. He had gone over the edge again.

But the ninja master would not be put off. "Or are

you afraid to discover that your entire life has been a mockery?" He drew closer to Hama. "That your entire life has been a betrayal of what you believed in? What you were taught?"

Daremo never actually finished the sentence. The words emerged, but their existence was cut off by Hama's attack. He shot the end of the metal pole in his hand at Daremo's sternum.

He could see the stick smash the bone from Daremo's ribs, collapsing it on Daremo's heart, rupturing Daremo's most vital organ.

Then his vision was paralyzed. Suddenly he was not in the cabin anymore. He was in a place with no walls, no floor, no ceiling. He was everywhere, and when that threatened to drive him insane, he was back, but not in the cabin. He was in the wood, with all the world stretched out around him.

Filling the world was the dead. And he recognized every single one of them.

Hama collapsed.

When he could see again, he was on one knee in the cabin. He knelt before the Ninja Master.

He looked up in shock. Daremo held his stick. Daremo's chest was intact.

Hama sprang to his feet and backed away from the roundeye in fear.

Daremo shook his head. "I didn't do that," he said with a small smile. Then, just to rub it in, he threw the pole to Yasuru. "He did."

Yasuru spun the long pole with his own pole, in a display of circuslike balance. Then he slid it into his one hand, alongside the thinner, shorter stick he already had.

"What is it?" Rhea asked either Daremo or Hama. "What just happened?"

"A Chinese mystic named Hui opened my mind to other forms of communication," Daremo described cryptically. He glanced at Yasuru. "I opened his."

"And I opened his," Yasuru said of Hama. "Just a crack."

Rhea looked at the jonin in confusion. Yasuru smiled and opened his mouth to explain further. But then she saw realization enter his brain. His mouth shut and his smile disappeared.

Rhea was on the mountaintop, the corpses squirming beneath her feet. She could not get a steady stance on the warm, pulpy flesh. The wind tore at her. Suddenly blood began to drool from every one of her pores . . .

As if each had been opened by a tiny, individual pinprick.

Rhea returned to the cabin, gasping. She found herself lying on the floor. Yasuru stood where he had been. Daremo was sitting on the bed, where he had first dropped the bound woman.

"Actions speak louder than words," quoth the Yasuru.

She looked at Daremo, who surveyed her sadly. The sadness was not necessarily for her. She opened her mouth, but had to swallow several times before she could speak.

"You were speaking cosmically . . . ?" she half suggested and half reminded him. He laughed, but did not get up. The demonstration had had its desired effect.

Daremo's face became pensive. "You were sent to help me and to watch over me," he mused. "Toward what purpose?" He looked at the Orientals. They had no answers and refused to hazard guesses.

Daremo looked inside himself. There he saw the horrified Brian Williams, the suicidal Brett Wallace, and the loathsome Daremo. The man who would lead a group of Americans whose only desire was to help others to disgusting, painful deaths. A man who would put a child in the way of a truck. A man who would destroy a woman's concept of love and a normal life. A man who would shield himself with the mind of another man, then shamefully, godlessly, abuse the man's body even after his death.

But he saw someone else there as well. A single, frighteningly alone man. A man who would always be alone. Who could never be anything but alone. He was the same as anyone—everyone is alone—except that he knew it. A man with no place on earth, none in heaven.

Daremo shook his head. "Who told you to kill me?" Rhea looked at Hama, who looked back. Daremo looked up, from one to the other. "Who gave the orders? The Hanshi? A Hanshi agent? A Hanshi representative?" The questioned were silent.

"Not the Hanshi," Yasuru answered for the two.

"Hama!" Daremo suddenly addressed himself directly to the yamabushi. "Remember what you said when we met in Central America."

The Oriental tried to remember, but all that was clear was the fight. All he could recall were Brett Wallace's words.

"'I'm ashamed of you both.'"

"'You're just doing the dirty work.'"

"'I'm not going to roll over.'"

"'If you're going to kill me, it will be messy.'"

There were other words—other accusations—but Hama couldn't focus on them.

"You said," Rhea started slowly, "you said 'the shihan was right.'"

Hama could remember Wallace's other words now. "'You are not executing me because of clan rules or honor. You're executing me because I pose a threat to you. Or, *someone else* thinks so.'"

"Was it the shihan?" Daremo asked quietly. "Did the shihan order you to kill me?"

Hama couldn't speak. All he could do now was remember their first confrontation in Central America. He remembered Brett Wallace pleading with him that he had been psychically attacked. The proof of that was now painfully clear.

Daremo just stared at the Orientals. He waited until he saw they both had heard his words. That they both had acknowledged them. That they both realized something was dreadfully wrong.

"Admit to yourselves that you could have been misled," he asked.

"Contact the Hanshi," Daremo said. Rhea's face revealed confusion, doubt, agonizing reappraisal, and hopeless indecision. Hama's face was intractable. He had chewed on what had happened here, but he couldn't make the final step into alternate action.

"You're useless," Yasuru sneered at them. "One cannot change and the other cannot decide."

Even the one-armed man's jibes failed to elicit a response. They were in mindlock as firmly as if Daremo still had the power. Now, without it, he had to do something to break the stalemate.

"What do you have to lose?" he asked savagely, standing sharply. "You can't kill me, anyway!" Hama's head snapped toward him.

"You couldn't even kill my student!" Daremo accused him. "You have to contact the Hanshi because the Hanshi is the only one capable of killing me! I won't die by your hand, or hers! I will only accept my fate at the hands of my master."

Hama's frozen countenance began to thaw and break. Rhea was shaken, her eyes moving from yamabushi to genin.

"Contact the Hanshi," the Ninja Master repeated softly. "Tell him I am ready to die."

9

In the midst of death, a precious life. A life, like a candle, which had to be nurtured and protected from the vicious winds. A life created amid anguish and self-hatred, but born of hope. Birth was the miracle of life. Death is only the end of the trick.

The kappa looked down upon the child, and smiled. The kappa stood in for the god none of them could truly believe in. Not after all they had been through. God destroyed millions of lives in his wrath, but was pictured as all-knowing and all good.

None of this for the kappa. The kappa was not all good and not all evil. He was not one or the other and he certainly was not both.

The kappa resembled a monkey, but had no fur. They sometimes had fish scales or a shell, like a turtle. They were not wholly malevolent, but they did love blood.

They would lure people to their deaths, but they would never break a promise. They had many distasteful habits, but they were unfailingly polite.

Rachel was not aware of the kappa's protection, or its uselessness. For the kappa was looking down, bowing its head—something a kappa could never do without losing its power. In its one weak moment of tenderness, the kappa had rendered itself helpless and impotent.

It had to rely on the meager protection afforded by the California hospital. They had taken in the mother and child without question, labeling the wan, dark, scarlet-haired woman indigent. She was put in a semi-private room to rest while the baby was cared for in the maternity ward.

It was all they could do, the kappa realized. He could not stay with the woman and child forever. The tengu and the Yuki-onna were looking for them. And, beyond them, the oni lurked. The oni were about.

The tengu and the Yuki-onna might take pity on the woman and child. They had, after all, only been taken in by the kappa. The kappa did not share secrets with mortals. And even if they destroyed the woman, they would leave the child. A newborn child could neither learn nor reveal mythological secrets.

But the oni . . . the oni would eat mother and child alive. They would chew on the writhing limbs and hear the screams as they swallowed. And they would smile their wide, evil smiles, blood running between their teeth and dribbling over their lower lips.

The kappa had to draw the oni away. The oni had to

be made to follow the tengu and Yuki-onna, certain
they were on the trail of flesh.

The kappa turned from the woman and child, sham-
bling away. It moved to the edge of the earth and waved
its arms to attract the onis' attention. It crooked its
finger, motioning for the oni to follow. It ran, hoping
the oni would give chase.

It went miles before it realized that nothing was
behind it.

Rachel slept in her darkened room, exhaustion win-
ning over worry. She had once thought that she would
welcome death. She had thought that many times in
the dizzying first few days with Yasuru. There was
nothing else she could live for, she thought. She had
experienced more than two lifetimes of love and pain.
Or so she thought.

And when she became pregnant, she wanted to live
just so the child could be born. Just so the union of
herself and her love could be celebrated: tangibly re-
created in an earth child. A child born of both physical
and psychic love. As the months wore on, she and
Yasuru had mentally communicated less—as if the growing child was drawing away the bond between man and
woman.

She was tempted, but didn't dare try to mentally
reach out to her child. It was too great a risk. Several
horrors had been unleashed by her bonding with Yasuru,
and then Daremo. She couldn't risk exposing an unpre-
pared, unprotected innocent to that. The child might
be born insane or autistic.

All she wanted to do was have the child. And then, if need be, she could die. But as soon as the child had been born—into the arms of the men who had conceived her, Rachel became desperate to live. Now she wanted to grow old, watching the child. Living her final life through her offspring. More than anything else, Rachel now wanted to die a natural death.

She knew she was exhausted, and that her feelings might change, but as she surrendered to sleep, all she could think about was waking up again.

She fell asleep . . . and dreamed of God.

He was exactly as she pictured Him. He was huge, but thin. He towered above all in blazing light, but somehow she could still look Him in the eye and see His features clearly.

Most of His face was covered by a long, flowing white beard, but she could see that His eyes were strong and deep, His nose long and straight, His lips and cheeks a healthy red.

He was covered in a white robe, a gigantic, gnarled, wooden staff in His hand. He was immensely powerful, but somehow still recognizably human, as if we had been made in His image after all. He sat in an invisible chair, swaddled in clouds, shaking His head as He hunched over. He watched what went on beneath Him, His expression one of frustration.

"I wish I did exist," He mumbled, tossing a glance at the woman. "Tangibly, I mean." He looked at her directly under coiling, thick, white eyebrows.

He straightened, stretching His arms out from one

edge of the sky to the other. "But the living God!" He trumpeted. Then He sat again, elbows on his knees. "No one understands," He mused. "Why should they?" He shrugged. "I wouldn't, if I were they."

Rachel said nothing. It was not her place to talk to God. She had a desperate prayer, certainly, but He knew all and saw all. Why verbalize—why wail to Him—when he must already know?

"It's only natural," He reminded her. "You know things as well. The yin-yang of this just didn't work She reared back in surprise. "Why should I be any different? I should take it upon Myself to do everything without being asked? That's rude, not to mention possibly inconsiderate, and certainly megalomaniacal."

He surveyed her surprised countenance. "How can you possibly think I am always right?" He queried. "I made you, didn't I? And see how well you turned out."

By "you" He meant all people. Rachel leaned over to look down at what He was seeing.

It was not nice. It was not pretty. Oh, there were millions of wonderful things, but millions of ugly, crawling things as well. The yin-yang of this just didn't work out.

Any evil marred the magnificence of the overall creation; like a drooling pus canker on a face, like a cockroach on a cheesecake.

The real problem was not the individual evil, but the wake the evil left. It seemed to spread and grow larger with each instance, infecting everything around it.

"You noticed that too, did you?" God commiserated. "It's bad enough. If only they didn't make it worse."

"Why don't You do something about it?" Rachel finally asked in exasperation.

God looked across at her, His expression one of hurt. Then He seemed to think about it.

"I don't know," He finally said, a little wistfully. "I suppose I've simply lost interest." Before she could formulate an angry rejoinder, He continued. "I have told you; I'm not different from you. When you make something, there comes a time to stop fiddling around with it and go on to something else. If I kept fiddling around and kept replacing you with something better, I'd never be satisfied. I'd never stop."

"Besides," He added. "You'd all be dead." He let that fact sink in. "Look. I'm always improving the formula," He said with a smile. "But not at your expense. The improvements go elsewhere . . . on other six-day wonders. And on the seventh day, I rest."

He leaned back, a smile growing across His face. "You know what?" He asked. He continued without waiting for an answer. "I'd like to come back. I really would. But only for three words. That's all you would need."

He waved His arm, picturing the event. "I'd write it across the sky in every language so everyone could understand. YOU ARE RESPONSIBLE. That's it. That's all. And bam, it would be Law. No plea bargaining. No 'the dog told me to do it.' If you did it, you pay for it. No reasons, no rationalizations. An eye for an eye and all that."

The Lord leaned back, tired and whimsical. "And

you'd ignore that law like you ignore all the others," He said gently.

Rachel couldn't think of anything to say. There was no defense.

"Live your life," God said, leaning close to her. "And just be glad I don't come back. Because if I did, I could get every one of you on something."

He leaned back, dismissing her with a wave of His hand. He had other things to do.

"You're on your own," He said. "Enjoy it."

But as she turned and walked away, she heard His voice a final time. Dimly, in the distance above her.

"And try not to make things worse."

Rachel smiled in her sleep and rolled over. Mrs. Buchanan, the woman with internal trouble in the next bed, lay still. Outside, some cars drove by, but the road was mostly traveled by tractor trailers—their drivers trying to make ends meet in more ways than one.

Outside the door, half the lights were out in the hallway. More than half the staff was gone. About the only people actually working the tile floor were the duty nurses at the duty desks and the custodians mopping up.

In hospitals, the janitors were not called janitors, nor were they trained the same way.

They were orderlies, whose specific duties were to keep the hospital supplied in the manner it was accustomed to. They moved around at all times of the day and night.

To the rest of the staff, they were invisible men. The

harried surgeons and doctors looked right through them. The nurses made requests and gave them orders without touching upon their personalities, and, often, their names.

To the others in the hospital, the orderlies were just bland, homogenized faces. That didn't mean they were white. Most often, they were black or brown. Or yellow.

The Oriental mopped the tiles. Third floor, maternity and "women's troubles." It was a quiet section of the establishment, with all the patients blissed out—either on drugs or the miracle of procreation. The nurses could sit behind the desks, drinking coffee, reading Harlequin Romances, *People* magazine or the *National Enquirer.*

In any case, they wouldn't be patrolling the halls, on the lookout for errant ninjas intent on murdering one of the recently pregnant mothers and kidnapping her newborn child.

So the Oriental orderly was able to just walk away from his mop and pail. He was able to walk into Room 3B, undo his shirt cuff button and roll up his sleeve, then to peel the tape off his hairless arm and remove the scalpel he had put there. He was able to pull the protective plastic cap off the razor-sharp blade and walk soundlessly past Mrs. Buchanan.

He was able to approach Rachel's bed, to lower the knife to her throat, and then to choke, his eyes and tongue bulging out.

He was able to feel fingers cutting off his air and

paralyzing his arm in place; to feel himself moving backward, away from the woman's sleeping body.

He was able to hear the crack of something breaking inside him; to feel the pain of fingers rupturing his internal organs, his kidney and spleen.

What he wasn't able to do was make any noise or fight back. The Figure in Black was too good for that. The Figure had come out of the shadows between the two beds, expertly mingling with the night so that the orderly's hall-accustomed eyes could not adjust to his presence.

The Figure in Black would not allow a low-level ninja—the single surviving member of the five-man team who had replaced Rhea and Hama during their recuperation—to delay or distract him.

He pulled the ninja away from the bed. He spun the ninja around. His arms moved so quickly the ninja couldn't see them. Five of the Figure's fingers were around the ninja's trachea. The other five were around his testicles.

The figure crushed both at once.

There was no scream and no emptying of the dying man's bladder.

The ninja stiffened and air was forced from his lungs in a long, low wheeze.

The Figure put one palm on the ninja's back, the other on the ninja's chest. He pressed both at once with amazing pressure. The ninja's heart stopped.

Keeping the same grip, the Figure carried the corpse upright into the bathroom. He changed clothes with the ninja. Checking both ways down the outside corridor until the coast was clear, he carried the ninja to the nearest gurney. He covered the ninja with a sheet and rolled him to the morgue. He waited until the room was deserted. Then he took back his own clothes and left the ninja naked inside an empty body drawer.

The Figure put his balled-up clothes in a closet. Then he went upstairs and finished mopping the floor.

As dawn drew near and the staff was at its most lax, the Figure returned to Room 3B.

PART FOUR— ONI

Ye shall know the truth, and the truth
shall make you free.
 —*New Testament* (John VIII, 32)

The descent to hell is easy.
    —Virgil, *Aeneid*, VI

10

Brett went through the bustling kitchen that was already preparing for the lunch crowd. He waved at Hama, their affable cook. Hama smiled as he kept most of his attention on the various woks and pots.

Ah, the good old days. Hama let his lips stretch across his teeth as he remembered the first time he saw Brett Wallace. He couldn't decide whether it was a happy or sad memory.

His facial movement looked more like a grimace than a smile. But he was leaning over, so he doubted anyone would notice. And if they did notice, he doubted anyone would care.

But others did notice and did care. Although to them, the line made by the man's thin lips was just another line on a round face with too many lines. Besides the mouth, there was the vertical line across the man's forehead, and the diagonal line across the man's face.

The men who watched did care, but they also knew the bald, incongruous man with too many lines on his face was in the one place where not many others would notice an extra slash or two.

It was about five o'clock in the morning. Mists of all kinds were rising from the cobblestoned ground. The mist of frozen breath coming from men's nostrils and mouths as they labored. Mist rising from the carcasses they carried.

A stench of pungent odors filled the air, with odors of life and death. The dead fed the living.

There was a timelessness about this place, a mixture of both rugged individualism and warm family feelings— family in the hundreds. It was only this huge family's feelings that warmed the cold fingers in the winter morning.

Hama was no longer lost in time. But he drifted through the present as if he were still buried in the ground. The sensations here had no greater meaning than his visions as a child.

Choosing the way now was just as difficult as it had been then. But he would not be crippled by indecision, like the woman. When he made a decision he had to follow through. Yes, he had been blinded before, but only to what his original decision had been.

With thought, he realized that his decision had not been to kill the renegade roundeye. His decision had been, had always been, and would always be, to *carry out his duty.*

So now he carried fish.

He was not alone. This was a place to carry fish. It was *the* place to carry fish. People came from all over the world to this spot *just* to carry fish. It was Tsukiji, the seven-acre Tokyo Central wholesale market.

They couldn't contact the Hanshi. There was no way of getting to him, no matter what or how or where they tried. There was no answer. None at all. That, more than anything else, distressed the yamabushi.

None of the established communication lines worked. The last man on the five-ninja hunting party was no longer "in place." That too was disturbing. Hama had told the man to wait for the yamabushi's signal. But when the signal came, the man wasn't there to receive it.

It was back to square one. It was the four of them alone—against the world. Hama couldn't kid himself that he didn't feel the exhilaration. It was the same exhilaration he had felt when the Hanshi assigned him to watch over the roundeye in the first place—many years ago.

After all the preceding years of indiscriminate, irregular killing (basically freelance executions of insane ninja), this sort of prolonged assignment was just what his psyche needed. And now, the thought that it wasn't over, that this too wouldn't end in the cold, ugly decapitation of a renegade, pleased him.

Hama corrected himself. At least *he* would not behead Wallace. The white man had promised that he would not fight the will of the Hanshi once he faced him. The white man might take his own life. Or the

Hanshi might end the roundeye's life personally . . . as a show of respect. But to gain his respect, they had to find him.

So Hama went back to his homeland. He donned dark green pants, rubber boots, a gray turtleneck sweater, and a pea jacket to get on the plane. It flew for almost fifteen hours before landing at the Tokyo City air terminal. The passport and visa offered little problem. A ninja, not to mention a yamabushi, was always prepared.

Hama got off the plane and disappeared into the market area.

It wasn't difficult. Tsukiji's seven acres were made up of a labyrinthine system of alleys lined with metal-covered stalls and surrounded by an ever-flowing sea of trucks picking up and dropping off. Hundreds of food stands and thousands of people crammed into the site every morning to scream at each other.

Hama was yamabushi—the warrior-priest—but he had been trained as ninja. He did what one of them would have done. He blended in. He *became* a fish pusher, a man in a T-shirt, pants, and pea jacket, hauling the fresh frozen tuna off trucks and washing the ice off the dozens of dead carcasses with one of the water hoses that lay around the yard like so many crushed snakes.

Steam erupted from the husks as if a smoke bomb had gone off inside them. The mist sprayed out as if the tuna flesh was wrapped around leaking pipes. They hissed, and the fish fog rolled in, filling the area with the scent of fresh-killed sashimi.

Eau de Sashimi brought the others out of the maze.

The flat-faced, round-headed purveyors came at the long lines of three-foot-long fish with their machetes held loosely in their hands. They marched down the lines like boot camp sergeants reviewing the new, raw recruits. Almost as an afterthought, each in turn hacked off the tail, hacked open the body, hacked open the head.

They twisted and tugged like veteran assembly-line workers, creating mirror image versions out of what used to be hundreds of unique animals. The subtlety of the creatures could only be seen by the people who marched after the purveyors—the buyers.

They moved throughout the open air store, looking like human versions of the fish. They all seemed alike at first glance as well—their white buttoned caps bobbing as they looked for the perfect meat tone. But then their fish hooks came off their belts. They swung them down like men on a chain gang. The long, curved points dug deeply into the fish carcasses.

They twisted and pulled until they could see the gut color, each looking for the perfect shade of red, a red that would declare tenderness and flavor. They searched with eyes as subtle as an artist searching for the perfect sunset shade of oil paint. They tore the fish flesh apart and shone their flashlight beams until the brass bells began to peal.

The auctioneers were ready to start. They rang their handheld bells until the crowd gathered. There was much to sell and not much of the morning. The fish had arrived at five. They had to be on plates by eleven. The men started groaning.

The voices mixed together like a church choir in intense pain. The red-capped auctioneers all looked the same, but they had to differentiate from each other in the chaos of the bidding. Jockeys did it with the color of their silks. Runners did it with numbers. The auctioneers did it with their voices.

Each bidding was as unique and different as are bird calls. The men would shriek, yell, howl, growl, bellow, roar, and shout—each priding himself on the accompanying, subtly unique hand gestures.

The buyers were no less proud. Their signals were also time worn and time tested. Each motion toward the seller had been developed and practically patented as the individual buyer's own.

The morning sale was in full swing when the first man tried to kill Hama.

It was simplicity itself: a machete to the head as the bald man walked away from the central marketplace. Hama blocked the blow sharply. He had no time to concentrate on his attacker before another machete-wielding man came at him from the other side.

Hama grabbed the first man's wrist and pulled his arm so that his machete blocked the second machete. A third man appeared in the narrow walkway to swing his blade. Hama pulled the first man's arm up so that it was between the third machete and him.

The third attacker froze. Hama's right leg kicked out, seemingly bounced off the third man's stomach and into the second man's solar plexus. Both hopped back, bent double. As they fell, Hama threw the first man across him and down. The bald warrior quickly retreated, then slipped into an adjoining alley as more men started hopping from behind the stall's counters.

They were not fish sellers. At least they were not *only* fish sellers. Hama knew because they did not cry out to him. There was no "Hey, you, what's going on there?" They were not going to the aid of their associate. They were attacking in successive waves.

Hama refused to let himself worry. He was concerned, however. The wave attack was popular because it was very successful. The waves wore the shore down. It lapped onto the sand of the beach until it was eaten away.

They knew that Hama would not cry out, even if he could. A yamabushi never revealed the ninja secrets. A yamabushi never asked for assistance. Even if these men were Chinese magician spies, the yamabushi would not risk revealing the true nature of his life to anyone outside the martial world.

So Hama had no choice but to fight through them. To fight through them all, however many. He pictured the seven acres in his mind as he walked quickly through the alleys. He pictured the seemingly endless series of narrow passages—like a plate of noodles with all the ends tied together. He could move among them forever.

So he had to fight toward the bank of the Sumida River. Although the water would be dangerously cold, it was his only way out. Hama glanced back. The plainclothes attackers were moving in and out of his view. One was always following him, but it was not always the same one.

They would interject, turn, twist, and retreat like a

precision marching band, going right, left, back, and
forth in Hama's vision. They sought to cut him off, to
surround him. Suddenly the entire world was the
hemmed-in enclosure of Tsukiji. The modern magnificence of Japan might as well not have existed outside
the massive network of sheds and sloping sidewalks.

Hama moved faster, his eyes searching for the one
thing he wanted. It came almost immediately into his
vision. It was a wrist. He grabbed it and threw the man
attached to it into the canvas-covered side of a stall.
The man shouted and fell, nearly knocking the loose
structure down. Others nearby went to see what
happened, congesting the walkway next to the shed.
That blocked one avenue for the attackers.

It gave Hama some room. It gave him some direction. He turned right, heading for the river. The next
machete came from behind, swinging at the top of his
spine. He ducked and kicked backward. The attacker
moved his torso, but that was not Hama's target. His
leg seemed to step down as it went back, hitting the
attacker's calf broadside.

The man's leg went back as if he were scraping
something from the bottom of his shoe. His torso came
forward and down. Hama reached over, grabbing the
machete hand and the man's chin. Hama's fingers were
claws as he threw the fellow in front of him just in time
to trip another attacker appearing in the thin mouth of
the alley to the right.

Hama moved quickly past them. Everywhere he
marched he heard the shouting of the auctioneers. It

was by their voices that he judged his location. He had little doubt that the attackers were doing the same.

Hama didn't dare wait until he had gotten sight of all of them. He had to institute a plan immediately. He started to run across the cobblestones. His sudden increase in speed drew one out. He chopped at Hama from an intersecting alleyway as Hama sped past.

But Hama didn't speed completely past. He spun, grabbed the machete wrist, and pulled the man into his kicking foot. It practically snapped the man's head off. Since Hama was holding onto his wrist with both hands, the man's body jerked instead of flying backward.

Hama plucked the blade from the man's limp fingers and let go. The man dropped to the ground like a boneless fillet. Hama sliced the canvas wall beside him. He leaped over the empty stall's counter and ran diagonally to the next cloth wall. He ran across the market, cutting through the stall's walls.

He could see the shadows of his attackers moving in silhouette in the alleys. They could see his shadow as well, but they couldn't be sure it was him at first. Only when they found the unconscious man and his empty hand did they realize Hama's strategy. They repositioned themselves to stop their quarry's progress.

Hama saw them coming. The canvas walls billowed. Their shadows grew and shrank in proportion to the sun. Hama stopped in his tracks, listening. He saw a machete blade cut through the cloth before him.

The attacker thought he had Hama. If Hama could see his shadow, then he could see Hama's just as well. Judging by the silhouette, Hama had to be in the middle of the next stall, simply waiting. And he didn't dare throw his machete, the man gloated—he needed that to protect himself.

That was the attacker's final thought before a thrown machete was buried three and a half inches into his forehead.

The attackers behind the dead man moved quickly back in surprise. They were looking down at their fallen comrade so they didn't see the shadow of the next stall nearly collapsing. They only heard the thin wood supporting pole crack and then Hama was among them, a four-foot stick in each hand.

He had torn a support from the corner of the shed. He had broken it in two and leaped through the slit the now dead man had made. He rammed one stick into the nearest man's throat. He swung the other at another man's head. The second man blocked with the machete blade. The thin stick was sliced, the smaller piece whipping into the man's face.

Hama dropped the sticks and caught the machete that was falling from the speared man's grip. He fought the other three off, using the knife like a wakizashi sword. The remaining trio backed into the canvas. Hama immediately retreated the way he had come. He dove through the cloth, somersaulting. He came up running through the alley, the machete held low.

He vaulted over another counter and went through another rear wall—the machete cutting him an opening. He could hear the others following and see their shadows as they closed in. He chopped through another wall and moved quickly down the alleyway. He could gain no more protection in the stalls now. They knew which shadow was his.

They came at him in the passages again. But now they were equally matched. He had the same weapon they did and he was yamabushi. No magician spy nor ninja dare be his equal!

Things had changed. They knew what he fought for now. Not for survival or success . . . but for his Hanshi.

He had kept them off long enough to reach the edge of the auction area. That, in itself, would not be enough. They could still kill him and blame his death on an accident. That sort of thing didn't happen all the time, but there were enough slips of the machete to make it seem acceptable.

Why do you think Hama's scarred face was viewed with such disinterest there? Many fishmen were scarred— many were missing the errant knuckle or a tip of the pinkie or two.

When a Japanese was missing part of a finger, an Occidental thought "yakuza." An Oriental thought "tsukiji."

Hama collided with a buyer. He embraced the man to keep both of them on their feet, then moved away, apologizing profusely. His attackers seemed to pay no mind to the crowd. They moved along the edge indifferently. Hama could see three in a group—the same three he had confronted in the stall.

He moved back into the dense alleyways, daring them to come after him. They took his dare. One motioned for the others to go into passages on either side, to surround and cut off the quarry. Then the first man went down the alley into which Hama had disappeared.

He walked into his own blindness. There was a flash of white that obliterated his vision. When his eyes cleared, they focused on the blade in his chest. But only for a second. After the light came the darkness.

Hama shone the high-intensity flashlight he had lifted from the buyer's belt right into the attacker's eyes. He stabbed the man and took the man's machete so he wouldn't waste time cleaning the killing blade. Then he walked quickly out of the alley and into the crowd again.

He went past the gesticulating buyers and sellers, heading toward the handcarts and weigh scales. Beyond those were the bulldozers, which cleared away the empty fish cartons at the end of the morning, and beyond them, the trucks, which delivered the bought goods to the next level in the Japanese chain of supply and demand.

The two other attackers ran from the alley where their third lay dead. They came quickly after Hama. The yamabushi positioned himself on the other side of the crowd, slowing, and then stopping completely.

One of the men slowed as well, surveying the scene for any sign of danger other than Hama. The third man continued to stalk his mute, bald opponent. Hama watched his approach calmly, his hands at his side. He leaned on a metal counter, rolling clouds of mist sweeping across his face.

To the man coming at him, Hama appeared and disappeared into white powder, accompanied by an angry buzzing that rose and fell in volume. But he didn't concentrate on peripheral sensations. All his energy was centered on his target: the infuriatingly adaptable warrior-priest.

The man drew near, his machete arm beginning to move. Hama's arm didn't seem to move, but the grappling hook in his fingers collected the man's other arm and swept it into the band saw blade next to him.

The hook had a long pole handle which gave Hama the mobility and distance to surprise his adversary. The band saw was hardly moving, but the sharp blade was enough to cut deeply into the man's arm. He opened his mouth to shout, but Hama placed the hook behind the man's leg, then pushed him—his first two fingers spearing into the throat.

The sudden fall was so surprising that the wounded attacker did not cry out. Not until he was twisting on the ground did anyone notice the bleeding man. But by then, no squat, scarred, bald man was nearby.

Hama was crawling over the bulldozer seats. He raced past the open trucks, throwing the machete beneath one as he went. He ran all the way to the edge of the river. He stood on the lip of the wharf, preparing to dive.

Then his body stilled. He stood on the very edge of the cement wall that served as the river's bank. The Sumida flowed nine feet below, cold and ominous. He looked down, all his other senses concentrating on movement behind him. He waited until he finally sensed something.

He spun. Before him were mildly curious draymen,

moving the fat carcasses of bought fish from the auction to the band saws. The fish were cut in quarters, and then the purveyors' machetes chopped them into slabs of slick, oily steaks which the draymen loaded onto the trucks.

No one was much interested in a solitary bald man standing dangerously close to the river's edge. They would rather talk about the accident that wounded a man's arm. They did not talk about a whole bunch of corpses among the stalls. Hama didn't doubt the bodies were no longer there.

They weren't coming. Hama's expected guests weren't coming anymore. The ocean had threatened the shore with a tsunami, only to deliver a coiling trickle. The waves had died quickly, hardly moving the smooth sand.

Hama couldn't understand it. They had him in a perfect position for ultimate slaughter. They could have overwhelmed him, and finally cut him down. But instead of overwhelming him, they sent in only a few men to destroy the yamabushi.

But there were many things Hama couldn't understand. After his experience with Daremo, he had decided to stop trying anymore. Instead, he decided to feel simpler emotions. Like insult.

Imagine! Only a dozen men to kill a yamabushi!

Hama didn't know that Daremo had already predicted this. That he had told Archer that there had already been too many deaths. Too many public deaths, at any rate. For the Moshuh Nanren and ninja, there could never be too many deaths.

But there could be too many bodies littered in public places to afford many more. Especially not in such a small country as Japan, where the crime rate for the year matched Manhattan's crime rate for the week.

Public slaughter was nothing new in North or Central America, but unwanted attention had already been focused in Hong Kong and Israel. The enemy couldn't chance a sweep of the Tokyo fish market—thereby risking the possibility that all the attackers would be found in bloody heaps.

They had plenty of time to plan for other things.

11

Rhea walked through a world she remembered but did not know. The Hanshi had sent her here, to Tokyo, before she went to San Francisco those many years ago. She walked as kunoichi now, blending with the residents, but the shock back then had been tremendous after all the years in her rural village and inside the walls of the ninja prefecture.

It was like walking down the time tunnel from 1868 to 1968. But it was not like going from the Dark Ages to the Renaissance. More like going from a magnificent ancient castle to a glass and steel disco. The realities of modern Tokyo as compared with traditional Japan were not so much bright as harsh—like a too-powerful light.

Things had not changed too much since then. The city was still overcrowded, apartment nestled on apartment, store on store like so many shoeboxes separated by tissue paper. Smog still hung over the city. The main reading materials were still comic books the size of telephone directories. The main entertainment was still soft-core violent porno films with such titles as *Red Rope Rape*.

Rhea tried to ignore the arguable splendor of the central section called Ginza as she made her way west across the city. White and glass ferro-concrete skyscrapers filled the cosmopolitan area as monuments to the country's modern age.

Once the architecture had been based on red brick, which were often compressed rectangles of earth and dung. The homes made of these bricks were lyrical and handsome. But the World War had literally bombed these places to hell, so most of Japan's major cities had to be rebuilt from the ground up after 1945.

The citizens who survived made a habit of it. Especially after the atomic bomb they prided themselves upon their patient politeness. They would breathe the smelly air and cram themselves into the blue, white, orange, and green subway cars without so much as a whimper. They would, in a word, adapt.

"Totonoemasu." It should have been the name of their main religion. It was, in a way. The fastest growing religion in modern Japan was Chuto-Hanpa, the adaptable religion. It could mean anything the worshipper wanted it to. The language was built around the same precepts.

In Japanese, the verb comes at the end of the sentence. That means it could be changed by the speaker at the last moment to amend or even completely change what he or she was originally going to say—depending upon the listener's reaction.

The city was not quite as adaptable. But if an adjustment had to be made, a person could always travel to the top of the Tokyo Tower—an Oriental replica of the Eiffel Tower (or was it the other way round?)—to see what it was all for.

There they were, stretched out in all four directions around the twenty-three central wards, the twenty-six mini-cities, the six towns, and nine villages that made up Tokyo. To the west were the mountains of Chichibu. To the east, the sparkling, only mildly polluted Tokyo Bay (proud result of a massive cleanup). To the north, the hills of Nikko. And to the south, Mount Fuji, famed in story, song, and video game.

And in the midst of all this organic wonder and nature's splendor was Tokyo itself, victim of progress. When the shogunate was abolished and imperialism restored, the country had to snap in line with the rest of the civilizations. As always, the Japanese based its future on the rest of the world's immediate past, taking what it wanted from each continent.

So far, they had been able to improve on whatever they copied. But the "improvements" were not restricted to only the more positive elements of society.

Rhea glanced at the headlines on a crowded newsstand's many periodicals. "Karyukai Killer Strikes Again," said the *Yomiuri Shimbun*, the world's most-read newspaper. Rhea shook her head and moved on, passing the window of a department store crammed full of tea paraphernalia.

The tea bowls on display were being packaged and sold like Cabbage Patch Kids—each one different and certifiably "unique." Dozens of different kinds of jars contained "matcha," the green powdered tea—"all specially blended to be easily whipped into a luxurious jade froth." At least, according to one of the tins' labels.

Rhea had to shake her head again, bitterly this time. Once the masters of cha-no-yu were austere, selfless people who thought only of spiritual pursuits. Now they ran chains of cha-no-yu schools, wrote syndicated columns, and personally recommended whichever tea paid them the most. Rhea felt itchy all over until she got out of the department store's range.

Next on the pilgrimage was the window of an electronics store. Crammed floorboard to rafters was a diorama of television sets, from one the size of a hardcover book with a screen the size of a camera lens, to one as thin and as wide as a briefcase. And a narrow one at that. The same image was on every screen: a talking head. And behind the talking head was a diagram of the sites where the Karyukai Killer had already struck.

Three women dead. In Japan, that was a breathtaking epidemic. They didn't have many murders most foul in the country, but when they did, they were increasingly shocking in content. A year ago, there were the murders of hitchhikers lured into the death car by a woman driver. This year it was the murder of women who looked a certain way and who lived in a certain section of town. All the victims had been tall, pretty girls with off-white skin and short black hair, who lived in the Shinjuku area of the city.

Rhea shrugged the silent news report off and continued on her way west—toward Shinjuku, where her apartment was.

It was more of a room than an apartment, really, and Shinjuku was more of a concept than a section. The concept was a particularly Oriental one: Let's see how many people we can cram into a phone booth. The hundreds of signs in this section were all tall and thin or long and thin. They hawked food, dance, drink, books, cameras, watches, films, plants, transportation, company, and good times.

The good times were on Golden Street where most of the bad company was as well. There were no green lights on Golden Street, only red ones. There a tourist could pick up something intangible which would stay with him for the rest of his life. It was the Flower and Willow World, "Karyukai," where anything was available if you had the yen.

Rhea longed to be with Miki Mausu at the Tokyo Disneyland, but Shinjuku was the best place for a woman to disappear. It was the old Purloined Letter ploy; to hide a man with facial scars, put him where scars are the norm. To hide a good-looking woman, put her where good-looking women were commonplace.

Sure enough, no one paid any attention to Rhea as she slipped into a narrow doorway in the middle of a street that was made up of narrow doorways. She opened the thin wooden door, covered with chipped green paint, with the slightly bent key, then made her way up the narrow, slightly bent stairs to the third floor.

On each mildly sloping landing, she passed a hanging piece of cloth that served as the door for each floor. Behind the curtains she heard children playing, crying, and laughing. She could smell laundry and dinners. The steam heat of both felt good after the cold snap of the streets. It flushed her cheeks.

The tired woman swept back the curtain to the third floor and walked down the angled passage between the individual rooms. The shoe box metaphor held firm. Each room was longer than it was high and outfitted as severely as possible without evoking Alcatraz.

The doorway to each room—four side by side across from four others across the hall—was where the residents' imaginations could soar free. Upon rental, each doorway was uncovered. The occupant could chose whatever portal he wanted—provided he or she supplied it him or herself. Almost everyone chose to flatter the landlord by copying the landing curtains.

Rhea pushed aside the cloth blocking her own room and went right past the icebox, sink, and hotplate on the right wall to the bed—which was beyond the tiny desk and standing cabinet on the left wall. The toilet and tub were at the end of the hall, shared by all eight rooms on the floor.

Even with all the opulent decor, living space was at a premium in the city, so any real estate went quickly. When Rhea had arrived, three rooms had been available. By the time she had settled in, all were occupied.

And why not? It had all the comforts of home, up to and including a tarnished wok on the hotplate.

As she lay on the bed, Rhea wondered whether it would be a good idea to change from her flat-heeled black boots, denims, and bulky oval-necked sweater. Naw, she decided. She didn't want to expose the long scar Archer had given her in Israel, anyway. The less she saw of that, the better she liked it.

It made a smooth line across her stomach, stopped when it reached her right breast and then continued for a half inch toward her nipple. Instead of slipping into something more comfortable, she only got up long enough to remove her long black coat. She rolled it up and put it under her head to use as a pillow.

It gave her a nice view of her outfit and accessories. She was decked out as a hopelessly hip young Japanese female punk—up to and including the fan she kept clipped to the double-wrapped ammunition belt. It went twice around her body (once around her waist and once around her left hip), the bullet cartridges flattened at the factory.

She lay back and closed her eyes, filtering out the sounds of the busy hostel and the bustling city beyond.

But she did not sleep.

So she was ready when the Karyukai Killer attacked.

He came at her with a cleaver.

He ran into the room silently, the cleaver raised. He swung it down, the blade biting into Rhea's coat. She had already rolled off the mattress, dropping onto the floor beneath the barrackslike bed's metal lip so he couldn't get a clear shot with the cleaver.

At the moment her body touched the floor, she kicked him just below the knee so hard he almost collapsed there and then. But he managed to hold out until he pivoted, before falling.

He fell to the damaged knee. Before it touched the ground, Rhea kicked him in his lowering face.

He sprang back up again, moving backward, the cleaver still in his hand. Rhea paced it, springing to her feet and running after him the few yards between the bed and the doorway.

He slammed into the door frame, the hand with the cleaver hitting the wall. Rhea still didn't let him settle. She grabbed the wok on the hotplate and threw the peanut oil, which had been warming on the low heat for hours, into his face.

The man was good. He didn't scream as the oil sizzled, making his skin blister and bubble like a pizza. Instead he held his face together with one hand and blindly flailed with the cleaver in the other, trying to cut her down no matter what.

All he hit was the hot, empty wok, which she held by the two handles and used as a shield. Then she used it as a club, swinging it into the side of his head. It actually made a *bong* sound as it bounced off his skull. He was thrown to the right. She swung it again, throwing him against the wall. She swung it a third time, knocking him out the doorway.

He stumbled to the opposite wall, obviously planning to regroup there, but in his oiled blindness, he leaned against the opposite doorway and fell right over.

When Rhea appeared in the hall, the men from the

other latest rented rooms also appeared. They were featureless forms in the passage, one near the bathroom, the other by the landing.

The one to her left raised his arm. In his hand was a small, inexpensive .22 revolver. Rhea threw the wok like a Frisbee at him. It bounced off the gun. She followed it with a flying kick which sent him through the balsa-wood bathroom door like a wrecking ball.

She landed on her feet, facing the opposite direction, as he landed on the seatless, backless ceramic toilet. She exulted in the battle, energized by her ability. After all the years of frustrating search and agonizing indecision, she was deliriously happy to kill someone. Especially someone she didn't love. And she didn't even *like* these guys.

The third man came at her with a glass of liquid in his hand. He threw his arm forward, still holding the glass. The liquid splashed out, heading for her neck and chest. She kneeled, her hands moving spasmodically.

The liquid hit her open fan as she turned her head away. The fan was held so that the stuff would splash over her head and behind her. She saw some land on the floor. What didn't immediately sink in, evaporated.

Then she danced. Only for a second, but it was a smooth, poetic, balletlike movement which twisted her rising body away from the liquid while twirling the fan so it held the bulk of the stuff without spilling.

She flicked it back at the third man.

He tried to catch it with the empty glass. He tried to duck away from it. But a solid fistful landed on his back and shoulder. He instantly contorted, a moan escaping his lips. He erratically straightened, starting for the stairs. But then he whirled to face Rhea.

His expression was tortured and obsessed. She could tell what the contact poison was doing to his internal organs. He started toward her, his arms out. He wanted to hug her to him, forcing the last of the liquid onto her.

She ran away from him. She ran into the bathroom where she grabbed the second man with her fingers by his eyes, nose, and chin. She clamped her other hand on the cylinder of the Saturday Night Special. With a spine-cracking pull, she threw the second man into the arms of the third.

The poisoned man's dying wish was to kill her. His will kept him from being knocked down by the nearly unconscious human battering ram. The second man fell to the floor. The third man remained upright. Rhea pointed her arm at him. The barrel of the pistol was an inch from his nose. She shot him in the face.

The third floor was filled by an angry crack, then the third man's head nodded backward. His forehead was blackened around a hole just over the edge of his left eye. He crumbled as red ooze began to drool.

Rhea carefully stepped over the two bodies as innocent bystanders began to appear in their doorways.

"*Dame des*," the kunoichi said wearily. "*Nai mada*." Don't. Not yet.

They didn't need to be told again. Two stereotypical Oriental reactions were hysteria and total objectivity. It seemed the cheaper the living quarters, the more objective the residents.

Rhea slowly returned to her door. She was halfway through it when the Karyukai Killer leaped onto her back.

He had burst from the doorway across the hall, swinging the cleaver. His face was torn and hanging. He had been driven mad by the pain.

He almost cut into Rhea on the first swing but his nearly destroyed eyes had not judged the distance right. He half hugged and half hung on her as she stumbled into her room.

She instinctively knew she couldn't throw him off, so she threw him over. She quickly bowed, grabbing for any part of his body, and throwing him over her shoulder in a coarse judo move.

He landed on his rear, still swinging. She couldn't kick or hit him with the cleaver slicing that way. She backed up while he stood with the speed and strength that only pain, fear, and insanity can power. He charged her again.

Rhea threw the fan at him. He chopped it in half. Rhea ran out into the hall, clutching at her belt. When he emerged from her doorway, the steel-studded ammo belt slashed across his face like a whip. Which, in her hands, it now was.

He reeled away from her, swinging the cleaver madly. She drove him toward the landing. As soon as he had backed out of the third floor curtain, Rhea hit him across the face again, effectively paralyzing him with the shock of renewed pain. She kicked the cleaver from his hand perfectly. It spun through the air, fell across the steps and stuck into the second floor landing.

The Karyukai Killer turned to retrieve it. Rhea tripped him. He fell all the way down the stairs, slashing open his side as he hit the cleaver. He bounced and crashed down the steps until he smashed through the chipped green front door.

The murderer had hardly settled—half in the hostel and half on the street—when Rhea jumped over him and disappeared into the night.

He was an apt, honest, and eager pupil. He grew both as a martial artist and a teacher. He stressed the Zen, Tao, and other philosophies of the martial arts more than the ability to break bricks with your head.

Yasuru smiled at the memory. Ah, but he was so much older then, he's younger than that now. Younger than his thirty-one years, but still much older. He left the same arm in several different places: San Francisco, Mexico, El Salvador, Jerusalem and Tel Aviv. But at least it gave him some character, some personality.

Now, at least, he could be recognized for something, even if it was his handicap. It set him apart. It was a tangible (or, more accurately, an intangible) reminder of his life's purpose. He was genin—existing only to protect his sensei.

It was not so bad a life. He had lost something, but he had gained something too. Like the really swell suit he was wearing and the neat artificial arm he had stuffed up the suit's left sleeve.

It was attached by straps, like a shoulder holster, to his torso. It was a fine example of better living through science. The last time he had seen any artificial limb on

television or in the movies, it was the torso version of a
peg leg: a single joined G.I. Joe doll limb that just took
up space.

But this baby had some decent mobility. He could
move it around even better than he could his dead
arm—when he had had it. It could straighten and bend
smoothly at the elbow and shoulder with a fluid effort.
The hand was removable, but he hadn't been able to
carry any artificial fists on his person.

Instead the present limb was shaped like a living
hand at rest. And since it was cold outside he was able
to wear a pair of driving gloves, to give his hands a
consistent look. Yeah, things could be worse. Hell, he
could have been hauling fish with Hama or hanging out
in a slum with Rhea.

Instead, he was waiting for the man, the main man,
in the lobby of the super-elegant, super-ritzy, super-
expensive Akasaka Prince Hotel, where a single room
for a single night cost twenty thousand yen, tax not
included. It was a forty-story edifice designed by the
renowned Kenzo Tange on the edge of the Meiji Shrine
Outer Garden in the Chiyoda section of Tokyo.

Archer sank deeper in one of the grand lobby's
padded chairs, idly looking over the magazines, news-
papers, and books the staff had placed on the tables for
their guests' enjoyment. Archer liked looking at his new
hand more than the fat periodicals with their thick,
shiny, full color pages. He liked the way his new wrist
disappeared under the clean, bright white of his shirt
and the rich, dark charcoal gray of the single breasted,
two-piece suit.

Archer gave no hint that he saw the assassins in the lobby. He just continued admiring himself. At first he mentally cursed, wondering how long they had been innocently maneuvering themselves amid the crowded foyer to get within striking distance, but then the self-recrimination was totally gone; overwhelmed by the fact that he did, finally, see them, and that they hadn't killed him yet.

They were dressed for the part, which wasn't surprising considering that Archer had come from the airport directly here... and stayed here. The first man was decked out in a handsome, fur-collared coat, and a three-piece pinstriped suit. He walked casually, but with the brisk, assured steps of a wealthy executive. He was affecting an Englishman's manner, from the top of his brown homburg to the tip of his bumbershoot.

Only the bumbershoot went out of character as the man passed Archer. The tip moved unerringly toward Archer's ankle, right where his sock emerged from his shoe.

Archer crossed his leg. The bumbershoot continued its pattern, seemingly without interruption, as the man walked past. But at the last second, it snaked back, shooting at Archer's other ankle.

Archer grimaced as he slid forward, almost having to pull the ankle out of joint as he got it out of harm's way. He jammed his shoe against the umbrella tip instead— right where the sole was attached to the black leather.

The tiny, poison-filled ball was ejected into the bottom of the shoe.

The man walked on, seemingly oblivious. Archer

leaned back, unable to stop the thin sheet of moisture from appearing on his brow. But he wasn't about to dab it off now. The bumbershoot's backup was moving in. He was marching right in the door.

He wore a heavy woolen overcoat. His hands were carefully and completely gloved. His scarf was wrapped so carefully that not a millimeter of throat skin was uncovered. On the coat's lapels was a fine, light powder.

The man brushed his coat front as he passed Archer. Archer grabbed and snapped open a newspaper, then immediately closed it again. Outward. The powder swept toward him, then was swept back by the force of the fanned paper.

The man didn't seem to dodge. . . . At least anyone idly watching would not have recognized it as dodging, but that's what the second man did. He carefully removed himself from the powder's proximity. For its part, it simply fell to the carpeted floor and completely disappeared.

The assassins were getting desperate. The third time had to be the charm. They jettisoned all the subtlety they could and attempted a direct approach. A man started toward Archer's general direction, seemingly intent on the spine of a book. Only it was not a book Archer recognized from the lobby. He had surveyed the room carefully and he was trained to automatically catalog things like that.

First he saw the man's eyes move up in their sockets so he could target Archer with his peripheral vision, then he saw the vein on the man's wrist extend.

Archer raised a book of his own, flat, in front of his face.

The tiny dart hit and sank into the book. Archer slammed the book back down onto the marble table beside him, garnering some angry looks from those nearby.

This is a five-star hotel, young man. We don't slam books here.

Sorry, folks, I had to do it. If I hadn't lifted and lowered the book that quickly, the dart might have gone right into my throat. Hanshi knows the mechanism in the spine of the other book was that powerful.

The sound of the book was almost punctuation to Daremo's appearance. Archer looked over to see him stopping in the middle of a step on the grand staircase. He looked pensive, but completely at home in the dark wool suit he wore in the sumptuous surroundings.

He completed his step and stopped again. Daremo looked across the lobby. He saw the assassins there. He saw how they blended in with everyone else. He saw how they moved around the army of his dead who looked up at him and waited for him to join them in the foyer.

He was about to continue on his way when he saw something else.

Everyone in the lobby was the Figure in Black.

To Archer's shock, Daremo started shouting.

"I have a piece of paper in my pocket," he boomed. Everyone froze and looked in his direction. "I am going to walk across the lobby now."

While everyone stared at him, Daremo then did

what he said he would. He walked right across the
lobby and out the front door.

The assassins went away, deeper into the hotel. Archer ran after his sensei. By the time he reached the
hotel steps, he was astonished at Daremo's brilliance.
After that announcement, no one would dare try to kill
him . . . or even approach him! First, they didn't dare
risk murdering him without knowing whether the "piece
of paper in his pocket" was a bluff or not. It might have
said "ninja" on it . . . or worse.

Second, if he had suddenly keeled over—and even if
he didn't have a piece of paper in his pocket—the
police investigation would be brutally thorough. Japanese
detectives hated cryptic deaths like that. The assassins
couldn't risk *thinking* about killing Daremo then, let
alone actually attempting it.

Archer reached the sidewalk as Daremo stood on the
street—on the other side of a parked car. The genin
leaned over the car roof to congratulate his master on
his ploy and report, but he never got the chance. He
wasn't able to tell Daremo that Rhea, Hama, and he
himself had been attacked, but had survived. He wasn't
able to say that they were now all ready to meet him
wherever he deemed necessary to reveal the treachery
and intrigue to the Hanshi.

Still, the young man had been trained in ninjutsu.
His mind took in information automatically. Later he
would play it back to himself in slow motion. The street
had been crowded with bicycles, carts, small cars,
narrow trucks, and motorscooters. Daremo had been
continually scanning them.

One little red motorbike cut out of traffic to roll near the parked cars. The driver was a thin, young, Oriental man with a long neck, wearing jeans and a leather jacket. He was coming near just as Archer had opened his mouth to speak.

The Occidental only saw Daremo's arm move, jerking as if he were throwing a shuriken into a passing tire. But he wasn't. The tiny, dark-blue automatic shot out of his sleeve and into his curved hand. The motion seemed to flow directly into a straightarm.

The motorscooter driver seemed to glide right in front of the barrel. He started to turn his head away and the handlebars to the right. Daremo shot him in the left ear.

The man fell against the side of a blue van. He slid along its side, then fell between cars. The taxi following ran him over. The car behind it jammed on its brakes. The car behind it crashed into its trunk, pushing the third car's wheels onto the already dead man's neck and knees.

Several cars and bikes behind that cracked up in a chain reaction. The two-wheeled riders tumbled over roofs and hoods. The car drivers started to emerge from behind their steering wheels, shouting in fear and anger.

Yasuru looked away from the pandemonium to question his sensei.

But the Ninja Master was gone.

12

Japan is an island. It is a dense green land floating on water. The cities are just bright glass and tin puzzles stuck here and there across its length. Most of the acreage is covered with rivers, waterfalls, lakes. They, in turn, give life to trees, plants, brush, and moss.

The Japanese once built their lives into the natural order of the world that preceded them. Their living quarters were temporary, delicate structures because the earth was their true home. And they worshipped the powers that created such beauty, trying to create an equal beauty for their deities.

The temples and shrines became the loveliest imaginable works of wooden sculpture. These were so meticulously created that they seemed to grow from the earth, and not rest upon the ground. The cities were just tiny blemishes among such beauty. Ancient wonders and ancient beliefs could hide just over the hill from the modern age.

The Chiba ninja prefecture was deserted, with only five exceptions. All the others were in place . . . or dead.

Daremo kneeled, head down, in the courtyard of the Chiba pagoda. His walking stick lay on the hard, dark ground before him, almost floating on the white dusting of snow. He had come alone, called by a force he had been following through the four seasons. It called to him still.

Daremo remained in his suit, his tie not even loosened.

Lying several feet in front of him were the three men who had tried to kill him and Yasuru in the hotel lobby. Their tanto blades were still in their stomachs. They were bent over from their gaping, bleeding waists. A single, small, dark hole was in the back of their heads.

"Throw your gun away."

He heard the voice clearly. It was not coming from inside his mind. He did not need to look up to see that no one was there. His left arm moved. The little automatic came out of his sleeve, but he did not attempt to catch it. It spun away, landing in the snow ten feet from him.

Nothing happened for fifteen seconds. Then the little gun shattered, pieces of it leaping in the air. The snarling crack of another weapon reverberated inside the simple, one-room pagoda.

Daremo blandly looked away from the destroyed gun. He emotionlessly looked up into the barrel of another one.

Guns were illegal in Japan. The sight of the sleek

automatic in the man's hand was an unusual one. Daremo recognized it, of course. An expensive HK P5 nine-millimeter, with an eight-round magazine. An expensive German gun. Only the best for the shihan.

He was the Hanshi's aide. He had been the man who was always by the Hanshi's side. Unlike the Hanshi, this man was tall and dark-haired.

"You've killed your shadow," the man said, framed in the doorway. "The police are looking for you."

"No comment," Daremo answered evenly, eyes half-closed. "Where's the Hanshi?"

"I am the Hanshi."

Daremo shook his head. "You are not the Hanshi and never will be. Where is the Hanshi?"

"I *am* the Hanshi."

"Even if the Hanshi is dead," Daremo continued flatly, "he is still the Hanshi. If he is buried, that is where he is. If his ashes have been scattered, he is in the air around us."

"Don't lecture me!" The shihan suddenly shouted, emotion flushing his face. "The *eta* cannot lecture the Hanshi."

Daremo remained silent for a second, his lips pursed. "If that is so," he finally said, "that is so."

The shihan looked down on him derisively. "Eta," he repeated. Unclean. Filth.

"Where is the Hanshi?" Daremo repeated.

There was a moment where the shihan was tempted to shoot him. Daremo did not worry. Death held no fear for him, now or ever. He had died too many times to fear it. He might welcome it, in fact. It was that realization, clear in Daremo's expression, that held the shihan in check.

"The Hanshi is dead," the Oriental said. "Long live the Hanshi."

"You will never be the Hanshi," Daremo baited.

The shihan bit. "I already am. You are in no position to say. You are not even ninja. You are eta."

"The Hanshi created me," Daremo replied. "Only he can truly say who or what I am."

"I created you!" the shihan announced. "I! Torii knew nothing. Torii created nothing. He was destroying the ninja."

Torii . . . the old master of masters who recruited Brian Williams and oversaw his retraining. The Hanshi.

Daremo all but ignored the shihan, the master teacher, second to the Hanshi. His face remained placidly unconvinced.

"He was not even a direct descendant of the ninja family line!" the shihan maintained. "Only I . . . only I was! He was diluting the line, weakening the ninja."

Daremo let him talk. That was what he was here for. All those years of moving the chess pieces behind the scenes; all those years of manipulating had taken their toll. Now that the shihan had succeeded, he wanted to talk. Talk to someone below him. Talk to someone to whom his words would make no difference. So he talked to the human garbage he had used. He spoke to his instrument of revenge.

"How?" Daremo challenged. "By training me?"

"He didn't train you. I trained you. I told Torii of the

prophesy. The superstitious fool. He accepted my words and told the others as if they were his own."

Daremo stared at the shihan, understanding it all. After his quest, the four seasons of his search, the understanding was instinctive.

"So I was *recruited*," the white man said.

The shihan smiled at the roundeye's growing awareness. "Now you begin to see. You were never ninja. You were eta."

"And what were they?" Daremo asked, glancing at the dead men lined before him.

"They were not ninja!" the shihan argued. "They were not of the line."

Daremo looked up, his eyes glassy, dull. "What are you then?"

"I told you! I am the Hanshi. I always was, I always will be. I am head of the line. Hanshi. You should be honored."

Daremo shook his head sadly. "You are not Hanshi. You are *shinkeishitsu*."

It was quite a mouthful, but the shihan started as if slapped. He was instantly enraged because he instantly knew it was true.

"The Hanshi would not speak to eta." Daremo spoke quickly, harshly. "The Hanshi would not reveal ninja secrets! You are shinkeishitsu."

He was a man unraveling. A man who was coming apart under the pressure. Daremo could see it in the man's eyes, the man's face, the man's posture. It was the most dangerous stage of deterioration—when a man was capable of anything, unshackled by morality or rationality.

"I am Hanshi!" the man yelled. "I have the eyes of god!"

"*Zankanjo,*" Daremo cursed back.

"Yes," said the shihan.

"You sacrificed the Shiban's parents."

"Yes."

"You raped the Tagashi girl."

"Yes."

"*You killed my family.*"

"Yes."

Zankanjo: the ninja code of action under which anything done during a mission was acceptable.

Daremo was silent. Everything he had been afraid of—everything *that had to be*—was so.

"The line is unbroken." The shihan almost prayed. "My family is in place." He looked down at the zombie-still form of the sandy-haired, gray-eyed white man. "I shall say this much to you, eta. You were well chosen. You have completed your task well. I will allow you to die with honor. I will allow you to choose." He aimed the automatic from twenty feet away. The barrel was pointed between Daremo's eyes.

Daremo stared down the barrel. Within it he saw his entire world. The tragic comedy of his life was clear to him now. The superhero who had fought for truth and justice wore big shoes, a painted face, cotton candy hair, and a red rubber nose. Bozo with a bazooka.

It was only right that Daremo had not known his enemy, that he had not seen the villain of the piece until now. It made perfect sense that the Ninja Master had fought an empty shell of a villain. What was one more such villain in a story with no heroes?

And what was one more victim? Daremo had killed everyone he was supposed to. Could he stop now? What was his choice? To die by his own hand or die by his creator's? The moral decision would be . . . screw the moral decision. There was no more morality. Not after this song and dance. The decision he had to make had to be based on something else. The only thing that counted now.

Perfection.

Not survival. Perfection.

That was what the shaman told him in Central America. "You are all men, a perfect combination of good and evil. You cannot reject one for the other. You must accept both. Strive not for survival, but for perfection. Do not fight for life. Life is already yours. Seek perfection."

"I will commit seppuku," Daremo said.

"Hara-kiri," the shihan corrected.

A death by any other name would be as ignominious. Daremo did not let the ninja's jibe distract him. He reached down and pulled the tanto blade from his long stick. It was seamlessly sheathed within the handle of the katana blade.

He put the knife in his mouth, his teeth clamping on the blade. It stayed there while he shrugged off his jacket. Then he pulled open his tailored shirt, leaving its tail tucked in the wool slacks. He draped the shirt behind him.

Finally he took the tanto back into his hands. He

held it before the left side of his stomach, the blade pointing at his waist. Being eta, he knew the honor of beheading would not be forthcoming. But he trusted the shihan to do a decapitation of a sort . . . with the gun.

The timing had to be incredibly precise, but so, what else is new? It was not so much a question of whether it would be done, but how it would be done.

He drove the blade toward his own middle. As the knife touched Daremo's skin, the pain went into his brain and out. Yasuru felt it and instantly reached out and tore the shihan's mind open.

And something else.

And *someone* else.

The shihan's army of dead did not surround him. They crashed down upon him, as if waiting to be freed from their hell. He did not see them. They were inside his shell with him. They all screamed and tore at him.

Daremo halted the thrust of the tanto blade and charged across the courtyard, running to where the shihan reeled in the pagoda entrance. The gun in the Oriental's hand was pointed at the ceiling as if he were struggling with an invisible adversary whose hand was around the shihan's wrist.

Daremo grabbed the gun and stabbed the tanto toward the shihan's trunk—aiming it between the ribs and into the side of the heart.

The shihan grabbed Daremo's wrist and wrenched his gun hand away.

The two men separated. Daremo held the gun. The shihan held the bullet clip.

They both threw the weapon away and charged each other in the empty pagoda.

They met in the center of the floor. The shihan blocked Daremo's tanto thrust and drove his palm into Daremo's face.

Daremo flew back, tumbling on the ground. He only stopped when he hit the side wall. He had to shake his head to clear his vision. He saw the shihan growling, his hands moving in a brutal, flowing pattern of internal strength.

The shihan gathered his power in a frightening dance. Frightening because Daremo could feel the power. Feel it as if the shihan were piling weights on Daremo's soul.

The shihan's entire body moved in the incredible dance of death: earth, water, wood, metal, and fire; dragon, tiger, chicken, horse, monkey, snake, falcon, lizard, eagle, and bear; the movement, the strategy, the spirit. The shihan had gone beyond his earthly muscles. The spark of Archer's mental attack had taken him to hell. And in hell, the fire was limitless and eternal.

The shihan screamed and charged him, his hands out, his fingers clawed. Daremo wrenched his body away desperately. He scrambled out from between the wall and the attacker. The shihan's hands went *into* the pagoda, ripping through as if the walls were cardboard.

Daremo stabbed the shihan in the back. The blade went all the way into its handle. The shihan swung around, the side of his hand smashing across Daremo's jaw.

Daremo catapulted himself away as the blow connected. It was the only thing that kept his jawbone on his skull. Even so he flew out the pagoda entrance and onto the ground. He hit the dirt, rolled, but his momentum was still too great. He couldn't find his balance. He slid across the snow, his arms windmilling.

Rhea, Hama, and Yasuru surged around him.

They had tracked and killed their own shadows—the single, shihan-assigned men who had been following and squealing on them. Then they regrouped and raced to join their sensei at the ninja prefecture in Chiba. They could not have come into Japan together. Daremo had known that. They would have been too tempting and easy a target.

As soon as they were attacked in this country, Daremo knew for sure. He knew that there was either a traitor in the ninja ranks or it was *the ninjas themselves who were trying to kill them*. The attacks had started on Rhea and Hama *as soon as they tried to contact the Hanshi*. Either an Em-En was revealing the yamabushi and kunoichi's whereabouts to the Chinese, or it had to be a ninja plot all along.

The shihan tore the genin's artificial arm off, knocked Rhea away with an incredibly agile front twisting kick, and drove Hama back with a simultaneous double open-palm strike to the scarred man's sternum and solar plexus.

Daremo leaped over Hama's fallen form, his katana in both hands. He landed on both feet, slashing. Incredibly, the shihan caught the blade almost immediately *between two fingers* and let the blade's movements twist him around like a boneless rag doll.

Daremo tried pulling the sword away, but the shihan's

thumb and forefinger held it firmly just inches from the tip. Archer threw his artificial arm at the master teacher. The shihan knocked it away, but it distracted him enough for Daremo to retreat with his sword.

"Nothing!" Yasuru yelled. No one needed to ask the question. He was trying to mindlock the shihan but the man was not responding. The psychic attacks were useless. There was no mind left to control. The shihan's barely repressed demons had driven his mind from his shell of a body.

"Where's the Hanshi?" Rhea cried.

"Dead," Daremo said.

Then all conversation ended because the shihan came screaming out into the courtyard. Hama pulled a tanto from one of the dead men's stomachs and joined Daremo for a defense. Daremo slashed, Hama cut, and the shihan swirled his arms, legs, and torso around the blades. He danced by the two, then whirled his lower body in a double-legged spinning roundhouse kick.

His first foot knocked the knife from Hama's hand. The second hit Hama's head. The yamabushi went down. Daremo came at the shihan from the front, Rhea came from the back, and Yasuru went at his side.

The shihan blocked Yasuru's iron-palm thrust and didn't seem to feel Rhea's flying kick to his back. She fell away as he slashed eight fingers across Yasuru's chest, tearing through his shirt and into his skin. The genin spun away.

The shihan deflected Daremo's katana with one front twisting kick, then drove the roundeye back with a front snap kick. Daremo jumped and tried to cut the leg as he retreated, but the shihan had already moved out of harm's way.

The shihan screeched his triumph and swung his arms. He ran to one side and tore his hand through the trunk of a young tree. He leaped forward and buried his fingers into the neck of a slumped dead man. He twisted his hands and arms and torso as he screamed, then tore the man's head from his shoulders, splattering guts everywhere.

Daremo looked at the shihan's back, where the knife wound was. The shihan was hardly bleeding. He didn't seem to feel it.

The shihan's face and hands were flushed. All his muscles were bunched and his veins stuck out like coiled hemp. Sweat drenched his body. He threw the useless head away, barking at the air.

"Drive him back!" Daremo ordered. "As one!"

The three rallied, leaping to their sensei's side. They all came at the shihan at the same time from the same direction.

The exact moves of their limbs and weapons were uncategorizable. The blades flashed among flesh and the limbs moved among each other without overlapping or obstruction. The shihan shrieked and shrieked and shrieked as he fought.

One iron-palm blow from Yasuru pressed into the shihan's side. He reacted as if it had been a pat on the back. He slapped the young man away with the back of his hand.

Hama's blade sunk an eighth of an inch into the shihan's thigh, then shoulder, and then his chest. The shihan didn't respond to the wounds. They were just bloodless slits in his shirt. He caught Hama's wrist, twisted, and then kicked the crouching warrior priest in the face.

Rhea's stiff fingers jammed into the shihan's temple, ear, and neck. It was as if the pressure points no longer existed on the man's body. She stabbed his eye. Her digits actually *bounced off*. The eye was undamaged. He slammed the side of his palm onto her shoulder and then swept up into her chin. She spun backward.

Daremo jabbed his sword forward and then up. The shihan raised his arms and bent backwards. Daremo sliced toward the shihan's waist. The shihan cartwheeled away.

He landed in the pagoda's entrance. He tore out hunks of the frame, laughing hysterically.

Daremo leaped toward him, throwing the sword.

The blade shot over the shihan's head. His eyes automatically followed it, secure that any kick would be useless. Daremo didn't kick. He flattened his body across the shihan's chest. His momentum and weight knocked them both down. Daremo rolled over the shihan and into the big room.

"Get him!" Daremo shouted at the others.

They aligned themselves in the pagoda entrance. If the shihan was going to get out, he would have to go through them.

"No!" Daremo cried. "Inside."

Archer charged directly at the smiling shihan. He stabbed his single arm forward again and again, letting the shihan's seemingly effortless blocks catapult him into another attack.

If the man blocked and pushed the arm away, he would execute a spin kick. The spin kick blocked, he would fall and try a scissors kick. The scissors kick deflected, he would vault to his feet and snake his arm in for another iron-palm strike.

Rhea moved to the right. Hama moved in from the left. They kicked and punched at him. He was a whirling blender between them. He was moving so fast that they couldn't focus on him. He was moving so fast that his sweat would slap at them, stinging their skin. His entire body was a blur even though he was in one place. But they felt his bruising blocks and jarring kicks.

He kept them off him for fifteen seconds. Then he grabbed Hama's knife. He held the tanto by the blade and then stepped on Hama's upper arm, nearly breaking the bone.

He threw the knife at Archer, hitting him in the face with the tanto handle. As Yasuru reared back, the shihan swept the genin's legs out from under him. He fell heavily on his shoulders.

He grabbed Rhea around the throat, his sliced hand smearing blood on her. Her own hands moved like lightning, pounding his ears. It must have deafened him, but he paid no attention. He was only hearing the howling of the dead. He hurled her to the floor, head first.

Daremo stood quickly before him, the automatic pistol in his hand. He had retrieved the clip. He had reloaded the gun. He pointed it directly at the shihan's head.

"Kill him!" Rhea and Archer yelled at the same time.

Daremo pulled the trigger.

The bullet missed.

The shihan was pure ninja, directly descended along the family line that went back a thousand years. He was the Master Teacher. No bullet could touch him. He could be wherever the bullet was not.

The shihan stood, glorious in his insanity. His teeth were revealed in a huge smile, sweat pouring across them. He breathed in ragged streams. His eyes were a network of scarlet lines. His jaw was clenched so tight that he could no longer shriek. The sounds were burbles and grunts.

Daremo tossed the gun to him.

Rhea began to cry.

Yasuru could only stare in disbelief.

Hama swore that Daremo would die before him.

The shihan put the gun in his mouth and blew his brains out.

The oni groaned and laughed and pounded each other on the shoulders and slapped the butt of their palms against their foreheads.

The astonished merriment went on for some time after the gunshot. They just couldn't get over it.

"Imagine the balls it must have taken for that guy to just throw him the gun like that," said a giant red one.

"He just tossed it," said a gray, three-eyed one. "Like

this." He mimicked Daremo with an exaggerated expression of disinterest.

"Man," said a horned blue one, "you just can't tell anymore. You just never know."

The oni shook their heads, made their farewells, put their mallets on their shoulders, picked up their iron spikes and went back to other business. They were devils, after all, and they had work to do.

They stood over the shihan's body, some the worse for wear. The physical pain they could endure. It was the other stuff that was killing them. The same stuff, ultimately, that killed the shihan.

Daremo would not let it kill them. He didn't even need a "What happened?" from Archer or a "Why?" from Rhea.

"He was a direct descendant of a major ninja family," he said quietly. "For hundreds of years. Inbreeding. That and the horror of constant killing must have created this monster."

That wasn't enough. Daremo turned and walked into the gray of the late afternoon. "He was feeling what the mystic Hui must have felt. Only he couldn't take it. He couldn't even begin to control it." Daremo turned back to the others, who stood in the pagoda doorway. "The same mental pain killed Brett Wallace."

Before they would have argued that he was still Brett Wallace. Not anymore.

"I would go anywhere to stop the pain. The mystic Hui had to live on a mountaintop to escape the pain.

The shihan had no where to run, no escape . . . except this." Daremo held up the gun.

"The Hanshi is dead . . ." Rhea half asked in a hollow voice.

"He must be," Daremo replied. "But he must have died a natural death. The shihan didn't dare kill him. It was through the Hanshi that he controlled the ninja." Hama looked up on that disclosure.

"But the Hanshi was old," Daremo continued. "Senile. The shihan hated what was happening to them."

"What?" Hama's sharp electronic voice cut in.

"They were being homogenized," Archer reasoned. "They were 'going straight.' The world could no longer tolerate an art of assassination. So it became the 'Art of Stealth.' The 'Way of the Shadow Warrior.' Ninjutsu was becoming a sport."

"So the shihan created a prophesy," Daremo said gravely, "which told of a white warrior who would save the ninja from certain destruction at the hands of the Chinese Magic Men. The Hanshi was superstitious. He took the information at face value and passed it down to the rest as law. The shihan picked me as well, using the Hanshi as his puppet."

"I don't believe it," Rhea suddenly said. Daremo just looked at her. She couldn't meet his gaze. "I'm sorry," she mumbled.

Hama suddenly fell to his knees, groping for the tanto in his belt. Daremo kicked it out of his hand. He hit the scarred face with his fist. Hama fell back, his nose bloodied.

"Goddamm it!" Daremo shouted in his face. "Haven't

you learned *anything?*" He spun around, looking from one to the other. "You want to die? *I'll* kill you."

Both the woman and the scarred man looked away. Yasuru went to retrieve his artificial arm.

"Yamabushi," Daremo continued calmly. "Kunoichi. You have been party to an evil, but not with dishonor. You only acted honorably. To punish yourselves would be an insult."

It did no good. Both were paralyzed by shame. "Listen to me," Daremo hissed. "You were party to evil, but so was I. The evil was directed at me, but at you too."

They looked at him in cautious disbelief. "The Hanshi was convinced that I was the ninja savior. He had to have me. But to keep me, he had to have you too. The ninjas sacrificed Hama's parents to secure his loyalty. They saved Rhea from a rape they had arranged to secure hers."

That managed to break through their shame. Daremo had to continue quickly, before they realized the full extent of their molestation.

"Then, when I would not join, they arranged the deaths of my family. My wife. My child."

"Why?" Archer exploded. He came forward, pleading with his sensei. "Why did they have to have you? Why did they need a white ninja?"

Brett Wallace was still devastated, but Daremo was proud of his genin. The man was stopping them from dwelling on their tragedies. The truth would set them free.

"They needed a white ninja so they could kill him," Daremo answered, almost grinning.

"The shihan wanted to destroy what the ninja had become. Brett Wallace was the ultimate example of what the ninja had become. The shihan had to prove to himself that the elements he hated would destroy each other.

"Once the Ninja Master was in place, the shihan discovered a terrible mistake. The Hanshi had misinterpreted the prophesy. The roundeye would not save the ninja, but eradicate it. Brett Wallace had to die."

"But what purpose would that serve?" Rhea questioned.

Daremo did grin at her. "The shihan had picked me well. I did not die easily." Left unspoken was the fact that the shihan had picked Hama and Rhea in addition. They had not killed easily.

"The shihan sent the good ninjas after you," Rhea suddenly realized.

"There are no good ninjas," Daremo said. "Only loyal ones."

"The ninja loyal to the Hanshi were sent to kill us," Archer figured in amazement. "And *we* killed them for the shihan!"

"Those that failed and lived," Daremo added, looking at the three men with bullet holes in their heads, "took the honorable way out."

The magnitude of the plot overwhelmed them. Rhea's and Hama's entire lives were mockeries. They had been sorely used, dishonorably . . . and honor was all they had. Brian Williams's life had been destroyed, the things he loved most slaughtered.

Zankanjo.

"Wait," said Archer. "Wait a minute. We missed something." All eyes turned to him. He was staring at his empty sleeve, the plastic and metal arm in his hand.

"The Figure in Black," he said. "Who was the Figure in Black?"

Daremo nodded toward the pagoda. "Him," he lied. "The shihan. He taunted us and led us to the strongholds of loyal ninjas."

They accepted his explanation. In truth, the yamabushi and kunoichi were classic "order followers." They did what their parents and the masters told them to. The genin for his part, was too weak and overwhelmed to think clearly. They banded together out of shared emotional and physical pain. They had a lot of thinking to do, and none of it concerned the Ninja Master's final explanation.

"Daremo," Rhea said.

He saw her expression, then turned to the others. "Go away," he told them.

Hama looked lost. Both his homes had been destroyed. In Japan and in San Francisco. Where could he go?

Archer stepped over to face the yamabushi. "Come on," he suggested. "Follow me." The one-armed man started out of the courtyard.

Hama turned to the white man helplessly. "Don't look at me," the roundeye said. "Start making your own decisions."

"Daremo," he croaked—his own, unassisted voice a

pitiful whimper. The yamabushi was sixty years old. He had spent his life dedicated to a master. It was too much to ask him to change now. It would have been cruel. Needlessly cruel.

"Yes," Daremo said. It was not a reply. It was an assurance. There was a place.

Hama followed Yasuru, the weight of his mistakes heavy on his shoulders.

Rhea stood in the courtyard, unsure what she should do. Daremo waited until the others were out of sight before going to her.

He put his hand under the neck of her sweater. He lay his hand on her shoulder. She felt the warmth of his touch.

"Rena," he said. Rena meant love in Japanese. "Rena, you are all I have left. And I cannot live with nothing."

Rhea Tagashi died at that moment, on that afternoon. She died with her Hanshi and the shihan.

Rena was born in her place. She exulted in the new life. As he had said, it was all they had now.

The year of the Ninja Master is not over.
It is New Year's Eve.

13

Katsura.

Where Brian Williams's wife waited for him in death...

The two Figures in Black waited for each other.

They stood in the tall grass, obliterated from sight. They had faced each other on the road, then disappeared into the field.

They waited each other out.

They were identical to each other except in two respects. One of them had his sword encased in a walking stick while the other had it in a cane. And one held the sword in the "Jigoku Aisatsu" position. Hell's Greeting.

They waited silently and motionlessly. They stood where they were for an entire day and half of another one. Carts went by. Birds flew overhead. The sun set and rose again. They still did not move.

But one of them was not ninja. One of them had celebrated his success with wine and song. One had gone forward to continue on the next phase of the Plan.

One was forced to urinate.

Daremo attacked.

He heard and smelled the urine and leaped to the spot. He chopped down the grass and raced after the running Figure. The Figure reached the road and pulled his own blade from the bamboo cane. It was a straight, two edged tai-chi sword.

Daremo pulled the HK P5 automatic from behind his back and shot the Figure in the chest once. With the last bullet, he shot the Figure in the head.

The Figure reeled back, his arms waving. His head jerked as if kicked. He fell to the mud on his side.

Daremo looked down the road both ways. No one and nothing was in sight. He pulled off his own hood and one-way visor. He looked down at the prone form. He stepped toward it, then stopped. He stepped back again.

"Get up," he said.

The Figure didn't move. The chest didn't rise and fall, the nostrils didn't flare, the veins in the wrist didn't even twitch.

"Come on, get up," Daremo repeated in disgust. "I'll wait until you shit this time."

The Figure slowly got to his feet. Daremo raised the gun, holding it by the barrel.

"See?" he said, pulling out the empty clip. "No more bullets. Might as well take off the hood. I'd like to see what you look like anyway."

The Figure shook his head. "I don't want you to see my eyes," he said in Japanese. That was logical. Daremo might be able to judge the next attack by the enemy's eyes. "How did you find me?"

Daremo shrugged. "In a vision. What's the suit made of?"

"An American discovery. Calibrake. You could have used it as well."

"Very good," Daremo nodded. "It can even stop a nine-millimeter bullet at close range."

"It didn't tickle," the Figure said.

"I imagine not."

They stood across from each other again for several more minutes. While they waited, Daremo thought.

The shihan had said that all the true ninja were in place. *In place for what?*

The Plan couldn't have been a closed circle. The shihan hadn't merely used the concept and the name "Liu Chia" to throw Daremo off track. The shihan hadn't used it at all. Liu Chia was one of the shihan's agents. They were in league together for the Plan.

"What is the Plan?" Daremo suddenly asked.

"Didn't the mystic Hui tell you?" the Figure answered sarcastically.

"Who knows?"

The Figure shook his head again. "I won't tell you."

"How about this then? How could a ninja team with a magic man?"

The Figure laughed. "It's only natural. Everything here is Chinese. Everything Japan is known for originated in China. Tea, bonsai trees, the language, martial arts...even the ninja themselves. We did not team. We were always one."

Daremo sighed. "All right, then. I'll tell you. The shihan wanted to return the ninja to its ancient ways. That couldn't be done by just getting rid of the recent recruits. The ninja had to become assassin-spies again. But there's no market for magic men in today's world. A hitman could infiltrate better than an Oriental—"

The Figure attacked in mid-sentence. Daremo countered his sword play, but had to back up to do it. He dropped his mask and visor. The Figure crushed it into the mud as he went by.

They flailed at each other with their swords, each blade singing when they clashed. They danced through the air. When the Figure went for his head, Daremo countered with smooth stanced defenses. When the Figure hacked at his feet, Daremo held the blade like a staff, blocking each attempt.

No samurai sword or ninja-to could have countered all the Chinese techniques, but Daremo had fashioned his own weapon: part sword, part lance, part spear, and part tonki. The Figure leaped and crouched and twirled, all with amazing speed and dexterity. His bones were steel, but his joints were rubber bands.

But a tai-chi sword was not a Japanese blade. Daremo maneuvered his opponent until the Figure jabbed at his eyes. Daremo swept the Chinese sword down with the wooden scabbard until it was halfway buried in the mud. Then he brought the katana across the steel's side. He snapped the tai-chi blade in two.

The Figure moved in close and swung the back of his

hand at Daremo's cheek. The wooden scabbard came up at the last moment to block it. Daremo felt studs dig into the wood, just barely touching his flesh.

The Figure had small squares of poison pins attached just above the knuckles on each hand. Daremo disengaged and retreated. The Figure came for him as "Nanquan"—a South Shadow Boxer. The Figure came in shrieking, crouching low with steady footwork, his hands twisting into sharp striking shapes.

The vigorous attack seemed to sweep Daremo's weapons aside. He needed his legs to protect his exposed middle. Finally he had to throw his scabbard away to free one hand. He hurled it far behind him so the Figure couldn't dive for it.

The Figure used the pin pads to block and deflect the katana edge. By the time they had exhausted that maneuver, the Figure's gloves were in strips. Daremo could now see the pins clearly. Each one was a tiny pyramid—which would make a puncture that couldn't be closed. The poison coating on each could flow in, unobstructed.

The Figure started to waver, then actually wobble. Daremo moved back quickly. The Drunken style of kungfu was the most insidious and versatile. As the Figure stumbled toward him, Daremo kept moving away. The Figure suddenly snapped rigidly into "Changquan"—a Long Shadow Boxer.

They lived up to their names. They cast long shadows by practically flying through the air. Their arm and leg blows were fully extended, putting all the power of the body behind it. The Figure's body spun, leveling the air with sudden kicks and strikes.

Daremo leaped, somersaulting, into the high grass to avoid the fists and feet. He emerged immediately, countering with sharp, continual kicks. His leg would flash out and the Figure would chop at it, but Daremo's knee was too fast. The Figure suddenly somersaulted below the leg and jabbed upward at Daremo's crouch.

The roundeye used the Figure's head as a vaulting point and flew over the Chinese's body. He tried to tear the hood off as he went, but it was attached to the rest of the suit. He had to let go as the Figure twisted below him. He twisted himself, and the opponents landed facing each other.

The visor flashed—as it had in Israel. Daremo ducked, but he had to wrench himself back as the Figure's legs shot up into his stomach.

It was the first strike. Daremo hurdled back into the tall grass, hands first. He cartwheeled, but the Figure was already upon him. His foot came shooting out of nowhere. Daremo swung his sword to chop the foot in half. The blade connected but didn't bite.

The foot disappeared and Daremo went after it. The Figure kicked him from behind. He had slithered in the grass until he had circled his foe. Daremo dove out of the field and fell chest first into the mud. He turned over and brought his sword up, but it was too late.

The Figure erupted from the grass, kicking Daremo's sword wrist. Then the Ninja Master felt it. There were steel bands in the Figure's shoes. They ripped the sword from his hand.

Daremo tried to slide out under the Figure, but the mud was too sticky. It slowed him long enough for the Figure to pound Daremo's chest and stomach with extended Hung Gar knuckles. Daremo collapsed in the mud with the Figure straddling him.

The Figure tried killing blows to the throat and the brow, but Daremo just managed to deflect them. The Figure's hands slid off the blocks. He tried to force his fingernails across Daremo's lips. The ninja suddenly realized the fingernails had to be poisoned.

Daremo's feet came out of nowhere. One was on the Figure's chest, the other kicked the Figure in the back of the head, forcing his hands out for balance. For a second, the adversaries' faces weren't more than six inches apart.

Daremo catapulted the Figure away as the stream of white powder burst from his face mask.

The Figure flew through the air backward. What should have been a cloud became a stream of fine poisonous powder. Daremo rolled away as fast as he could, but he couldn't prevent the first few grains from reaching his face.

Daremo catapulted up to discover that his brain had become oatmeal. The poison attacked his neural centers. He had not gotten anything close to a deadly dose, but even the few granules sinking into his flesh were enough to make his mind fill with mush.

The Figure exulted, attacking explosively with his most devastating style. He was "Franziquan"—the Eight Attack Boxer. He flowed from one posture to the next, his blows striking Daremo at lightning speed. He pounded every inch of Daremo's front, breaking his nose, splitting his lips, and cracking three ribs.

He smashed Daremo in the side of the head with his iron-swathed foot. Daremo felt like his skull was being torn from his spine. He didn't even feel himself going five feet in the air or landing heavily on his back.

He lay half in the grass and half on the road. His legs and hands were in the mud. His vision was clearing and his senses sharpening but it was too late. The Figure wouldn't take time to gloat. He didn't need to. He had been, was, and always would be the superior warrior.

His black, featureless visage stared down at Daremo, his right hand cocked for the final blow.

"Your face," Daremo begged.

The Figure shook his head.

Daremo threw a fistful of mud against the visor.

The Figure struck. Daremo jerked his head aside. The blow glanced off his ear.

The Figure tore his obscured visor off. Daremo could see his brown eyes. To his shock, they were nothing. They didn't gleam, they didn't shine, they weren't piercing. The Figure had tiny little pig eyes under puffy lids.

Daremo smiled weakly. This discovery would have to do.

What strength he had left had been expended by the mud, the head twisting, and the smile. The Figure raised his hand.

Scream

Daremo screamed at the top of his lungs.

The Figure in Black chopped the Figure in Black's head off.

Double exposure.

Daremo had heard the words in his mind.

But he thought he couldn't do that anymore.

Suddenly he had the strength to scream, and clearly see *another* Figure in Black appear from the reeds. His samurai sword sliced right through Liu Chia's neck. The Figure in Black's head rolled into the muddy road.

Daremo's hands shot out, the palms blasting the decapitated body away from him. He vaulted to his feet. It was as if the Chinaman's death had rejuvenated him. But he instinctively knew that the drug was fast-acting and fast-fading... when not fatal.

The other Figure in Black ran across the field, his bloody sword dripping onto the grass. The dead head was encrusted with black goo. The neck pumped blood into the dirt several feet away.

Daremo quickly retrieved his sword and ran to the severed head. With one quick slice he chopped open the mask without breaking the skin beneath (as if that mattered anymore).

He saw Liu Chia's face. It was meaningless. It made no difference. It was just a Chinese face—one of millions.

Daremo looked away. The other Figure was gone. That made no difference, either. Daremo knew where to find him.

Owari No Hi: Toshi No Ninja Master

Mas Yamaguchi was waiting for him by the cliff's edge—where Brian Williams' wife, Kyoko, always was in the dreams.

The same cliff. The exact same cliff.

The first Ninja Master, who was also the second Figure in Black, still wore his black mask.

"The woman and her daughter are safe," were his first words to his student in six years. "I saw to that."

Daremo stood nearby, contemplating the beauty of their surroundings. The sea crashed against the rock face hundreds of feet below. The ocean stretched over the horizon. The sky stretched down to meet it. The cliffs continued for miles in either direction, but Daremo knew where Kyoko Williams had stood.

"Master Torii said I would never see him again," he said mildly. "And he was right. I never did."

Daremo had known exactly where on the cliffs to find his mentor. His mentor Yamaguchi had called him here . . . as he had called him to Central America and the Middle East before that.

"The Hanshi was driven mad by Hui's attack," Yamaguchi said. "I was next, but it did not kill me."

"I know," Daremo interrupted. "I felt it too."

"I made you feel it," said the second Figure in Black. "It was me."

"Master," Daremo started.

"I told you before. No more master or teacher now. You are . . ."

Yamaguchi faltered. Those had been his last words to the second Ninja Master—the one he had trained and retrained—when they last parted. Only then, the sensei had finished, saying "you are one of us." He did not say that now.

"Yes?" Daremo asked.

Yamaguchi turned away. He looked out to sea. He looked out to see. "I led you to them," he said. "I took on the guise of their main agent. I trained you further. I tested you. I warned you of their weapons. I protected your . . . family."

"*Watashi wakarimasu,*" Daremo said. I understand.

It made no difference to Master Yamaguchi. He had his own demons to fight. His own oni. When he spoke again, his voice was tortured. "I was part of it, Williams-san. It was I who recruited you. I killed your wife. I killed your—" he choked—"child."

Daremo knew it was true and knew it was not true. He had not killed the family himself, nor had he arranged for them to die personally. But he was party to it. He knew what had happened and still he trained Brett Wallace . . . twice.

"Zankanjo," Daremo said.

Yamaguchi nodded. He, like Brett Wallace, had trusted the ninjas to be honorable, noble, selfless warriors. He trusted this mission to ultimately be positive in effect. He was loyal to the ninja as only a Japanese could be. It was his "face," his honor, his soul at stake. To admit he had chosen . . . unwisely . . . would be to surrender the soul.

"The truth was revealed to me," he confessed, for that is what this was. A confession of guilt. "I swore not to die until the wrong had been avenged."

"No!" The word tore itself from Daremo's throat. He had to say it even though he knew it was wrong.

"Yes," Yamaguchi answered with conviction. "For it is not over. You must rise from my ashes stronger, more certain than ever before."

"Certain?" Daremo echoed. After all this? "Certain of what?"

Yamaguchi looked directly at him, the visor off the black hood. "Have I not shown you all there is for man to know? Have you not seen Time's Seven Sons? Have you not seen The Cloaked One and heard the Psalm of David? Have you not met Lord Guan?"

Daremo looked to his sensei in confusion. He remembered them all—from the Season of Lava where the Dragon rose, from the Season of Sand with the

Lion's fire, to the Season of Woman where he had to gaze into the Serpent's eye. But he did not know what they meant.

"You have died many times, 'watashi no shinzo,' " Yamaguchi said kindly. "You must live again a final time."

Daremo nodded. This he knew. The true ninjas, the shihan's family, were in place, the Moshuh Nanren and the Ninja one. To prosper, to flourish, they needed a conflict. Not one where the world exploded in flames, but one where the fire smoldered, where warrior fought warrior and warlord faced warlord.

This was the Plan.

"You must live on," said Yamaguchi. "You must fight the battle within yourself. The battle is always within yourself. You must fight and win." He saw that Daremo was seeing the truth of his words.

"You, and all your family, " he finished forever.

Daremo looked at his master in surprise. He heard the name in his mind. It was the name of a woman.

A woman with ivory needles.

Mas Yamaguchi stepped off the edge of the cliff.

Daremo lunged for him. His body fell off the cliff edge, his arm reached down. His fingers sunk into something.

Master!

Daremo called to him.

I understand

But he heard nothing more, in his mind or ears, save for the roar of the sea.

He pulled his arm up. In his hand was a black mask.

His sensei had showed him every belief human beings held. The Mayan gods and the gods of the Bible and the Koran. The deities of China, the lords of Japan. He showed them to his student, his son, his self, in all their inadequacy and injustice.

He had shown him the power and perversion of faith and belief. He had shown him what happened when people fought and died for something other than themselves.

The moral of his life was: Don't make things worse. The theme: Take responsibility.

Daremo stood with a black mask clutched in his hand.

He sensed something. He looked behind him.

The army of his dead stared at him.

Then, without a word, they turned and walked away.

"It matters not how strait the gate,
How charged with punishments the scroll,
I am the master of my fate:
I am the captain of my soul."

W. E. Henley